"Nicky's memory of his father and his relationship with you are all blended together right now. He's confused."

"Believe me, I'm aware of that," Vance said in a sober tone. "Once you're back in Florida, your nephew will get it all straightened out in his mind. For the time being, it won't hurt if he's a little mixed up. I'd rather he clung to me emotionally while I take him up on El Capitan in the morning."

Rachel should have realized Vance had a reason for everything he did. If she was having a problem with his plans, it appeared that had something to do with her overwhelming attraction to him.

Her moist eyes searched his for a timeless moment. "I'll never be able to thank you enough for what you've done for Nicky. You're a remarkable man."

On impulse she kissed his hard jaw, then reached for her purse and hurried out of the kitchen.

Dear Reader,

Harlequin American Romance is celebrating sixty years of providing endless reading pleasure to its readers. I believe I'm their number one fan, and I offer my thanks and congratulations!

More than thirty years ago I picked up my first Harlequin novel and was hooked from the first page by the unique presentation of a love story that concentrated on the hero and heroine. It was set in Japan. The way it was written was so romantic, it thrilled me to pieces and I automatically went out to buy a ton more Harlequin books.

That sealed my fate. I ended up reading everything I could get my hands on. The stories took me to every continent and I learned so much. One day when I couldn't get to the store and was dying to read another one, I sat down and wrote my first Harlequin love story with pencil and paper. I placed it in Kenya. It became my first Harlequin novel, published in 1988, entitled *Blind to Love*.

Would you believe that in this diamond jubilee year, my latest Harlequin American Romance novel, entitled *The Chief Ranger*, represents 100 plus books? It takes place in Yosemite National Park in California, one of my favorite places on earth. As you can see, whether I read them or write them, I'm hooked on Harlequin books and always will be. Thank heaven for them!

Enjoy!

Rebecca Winters

The Chief Ranger
Rebecca Winters

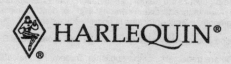

TORONTO • NEW YORK • LONDON
AMSTERDAM • PARIS • SYDNEY • HAMBURG
STOCKHOLM • ATHENS • TOKYO • MILAN • MADRID
PRAGUE • WARSAW • BUDAPEST • AUCKLAND

Recycling programs
for this product may
not exist in your area.

ISBN-13: 978-0-373-75265-2

THE CHIEF RANGER

www.eHarlequin.com

Printed in U.S.A.

ABOUT THE AUTHOR

Rebecca Winters, whose family of four children has now swelled to include three beautiful grandchildren, lives in Salt Lake City, Utah, in the land of the Rocky Mountains. With canyons and high alpine meadows full of wildflowers, she never runs out of places to explore. They, plus her favorite vacation spots in Europe, often end up as backgrounds for her romance novels, because writing is her passion, along with her family and church. Rebecca loves to hear from readers. If you wish to e-mail her, please visit her Web site at www.cleanromances.com.

Books by Rebecca Winters

This book, *The Chief Ranger*,
is dedicated to my adorable grandsons
Billy and Matthew, both of whose attributes
form the character of the six-year-old boy
in this love story. Nicky Darrow is as precious
as my own grandsons. I laughed and cried
while writing this book. It's very close to my heart
and was a labor of love.

Chapter One

"…And in the name of Almighty God, we dedicate the final resting place of Dorothy Twitchell Rossiter. We pray it will be protected from the elements until the day she will rise and come forth in the resurrection of the just. Amen."

Amen.

Vance Rossiter tipped back his dark head to take in the June sky. Brilliant white pillow clouds kept changing shape as they moved through a sea of blue peculiar to Yosemite. Maybe it was the trees in the park knifing into the rarified atmosphere that produced that intense color. This was his grandmother's favorite kind of day. Warm, with a refreshing breeze.

Content that she'd gone on to join his grandfather in a happier place, Vance chatted quietly with friends of his parents and grandparents. The fourth Rossiter had now been buried in the cemetery. They were a family well loved in this little community of Oakhurst, California, his birthplace.

Little by little the assembled group grew smaller. The hearse drove away. He shook hands with an official from the Sierra Phone Company, his grandfather's long-time employer. After saying goodbye to the pastor and the hospice people who'd cared for his grandmother over the last three months, Vance turned to his best friend, Chase Jarvis.

"Thanks for being with me today. It means a lot."

Chase clamped a hand on his shoulder. "Where else would I be?"

Vance gazed at his second-in-command. In a crisis or otherwise, Chase was the man to look to. "Running the park?" With both of them absent for the day, the chief of security was in charge.

A lopsided smile broke out on his face. "The guys at headquarters have everything in hand. They've planned dinner for you at Shane and Lisa's."

Vance glanced at his watch. It was ten after three. With the crowds of summer tourists descending on the park, it would take close to two hours to get back to Yosemite Village from here. "We'd better leave now."

By tacit agreement the two men left the flower-filled grave site and maneuvered their tall bodies between the tombstones to Vance's black Mazda, parked along the side of the road. Once they'd taken off, he said, "It was strange sitting in a church pew and knowing I'm the last Rossiter alive."

Chase's gray eyes shone with compassion. "I can only imagine how that must feel."

"*Empty* is the word that comes to mind." Even though his grandmother hadn't known him toward the end, she'd still been alive. The connection had been there. Her skin had felt warm; her fingers had squeezed his when he'd talked to her, working to a response.

He purposely drove past the home where he'd lived with his grandparents after his parents had been killed. There was a red Honda Civic in the driveway.

"The new renters?"

Vance nodded. "I'm glad someone answered the ad so fast. We agreed on a six-month lease. I'd have liked it to be a year's contract, but that was wishful thinking."

"Maybe they'll enjoy the area so much they'll stay on."

"Maybe. I should be glad it's not going to sit empty. My grandmother would be happy, too."

As they approached the Arch Rock entrance to the park, only thirteen miles from Oakhurst, Chase murmured, "Are you okay?"

"Yes. She and my grandfather both lived a full life and were ready to go when their time came. I can deal with that." He nodded to Ranger Thompson, who was manning the station, as they passed on through. The younger man smiled and waved.

After college Vance had joined the marines. He'd seen death up close and had dealt with it as it came, even his wife's. His red-haired Katy had signed up for the military as a nurse. They'd met and married in Germany. Their brief, eighteen-month marriage had ended when she'd been deployed to the Middle East and her convoy had been taken out by a roadside bomb. Casualties of war were inevitable, but devastating when they struck down one's own spouse.

All that had happened five years ago. Since then he'd gotten out of the military and had worked at two national parks before he'd been made chief ranger here. His marriage had been more like a series of short honeymoons interrupted by war. He and Katy had been incredibly happy, but fate hadn't allowed them to put down roots and start a family. At times the sadness came back, but Vance had managed to put the worst of it behind him.

He was doing all right now. The trick was to stay away

from emotional entanglements. In the end it avoided the kind of heartache he never wanted to feel again.

"There've only been two deaths that still haunt me," he muttered. The image from the helicopter, of a man's and woman's frozen bodies partially buried in the snow on top of El Capitan, never left his mind.

Chase breathed in sharply. "It wasn't your fault. You need to get over that."

"You mean the way *you've* gotten over it?"

"Touché," he said in a quiet voice. "But after I issued the warning, you weren't responsible for the couple. They refused to come down off the mountain."

"That's not true. Providing for the safety of park visitors ultimately rests with me. When you put out the storm alert, I should have had the Darrows ordered off."

"You mean the way the government orders people to evacuate during a hurricane? Some individuals just won't do it. They think they're immortal. We can't use force."

A self-deprecating sound escaped Vance's lips. "Another time I will."

Chase stirred restlessly. "So will I. It'll mean a lawsuit slapped against us so fast, Superintendent Noyes will demand our heads."

"True, but being fired isn't the worst thing that could happen, with two lives at stake. The Darrows left a child homeless." Therein lay the sin.

"Agreed. Let's hope a situation like that never happens again. I was here before you were transferred from Bryce. Believe me, Vance, you were sorely needed. In fact, you're the best thing that's ever happened to this park. Let's keep it that way."

"You're full of it, but I appreciate your willingness to go down with me if it comes to that."

Chase put on his sunglasses. "I agree the Darrow accident was a tragedy, but those two were the ones at fault for doing something so selfish. I know parents who fly separately when they have to travel. If anything happened to one of them, the other would still be there to take care of the children. But not every couple thinks that way. You can't be everyone's conscience, Vance."

That's what the psychiatrist provided by the department had told him in therapy. It still didn't remove the sting of guilt or his anger over the senseless death that had robbed a youngster of his parents. They had no idea how lucky they were to have had a child at all. Vance would have given anything for the privilege....

"You're right." Still, his hands tightened on the steering wheel, causing his wedding ring to bite into his skin. He hadn't taken it off, because a wedding band on a man of thirty-five in his kind of work was a subtle indicator of stability.

Not liking the direction of his thoughts, he phoned dispatch for an update. Cindy was on duty. So far, no emergencies.

"Sorry about your grandmother, Chief. I would have been at the funeral if I hadn't had to cover for Ranger Baird at the last minute."

"I know that. What happened to him?"

"The flu hit him hard. He's home doing you know what, sir."

"Afraid I do. Thanks for not giving me chapter and verse." She laughed before he hung up. It resounded in the cab. Vance flicked his gaze to Chase. "Our newest transfer ranger from the Smokies is cute and single."

"I was going to tell you the same thing. However,

even with that drawl I'm afraid cute doesn't cut it for me. But then neither does naughty and available."

Vance groaned. He could relate. "We're both getting too crusty in our old age." His divorced friend's thirty-fourth birthday would be coming up in August. Unlike Vance, he didn't seem to have any gray hairs among the brown yet.

"If you mean the park has become bachelor haven, you must have been cornered by Lisa."

"Lisa and Phyllis," Vance muttered.

"Add Nancy over at the restaurant to the list."

"Yup. All the happily married ones."

"Maybe."

"Careful, Chase. Your cynicism is showing."

"We're both a case for the books."

"You've got that in one."

DR. JOEL KARSH DIDN'T have a receptionist. He made his own appointments. Rachel Darrow entered the empty reception room outside his private office. After half a dozen visits, she knew to knock on the inner door to let him know she'd arrived.

"Come in, Rachel."

Over the past few months she'd been seeing the highly recommended Miami child psychiatrist often enough to feel they had a rapport. That was good because she was in desperate need of help from an expert.

"Thanks for fitting me in on such short notice."

"You said Nicky's nightmares are getting worse."

"Much worse since he found out I've got to leave on another cruise next week. I thought that was behind us. He's at the point where he doesn't want to go to bed for fear he'll dream. With kindergarten over, he won't leave the house or play with friends. He clings to me. My parents and I have tried everything to reassure him, but it's no use."

The psychiatrist sat forward. "I'm going to tell you the same thing I've told you all along. Since your father's poor health won't permit him to travel, and your mother has to nurse him, my advice would be for you to take Nicky to Yosemite and let him see the place where the accident happened.

"Ask one of the park authorities to talk to him and explain why his parents died. If Nicky can get his questions answered by someone who was there, it will settle his mind enough so he can let go of his fear."

"You really think that will help?" Rachel asked doubtfully.

"Medication can sedate him enough to make him sleep, but the real problem lies in his subconscious, where nothing in his world has been resolved. There's a reason for his terror. He was staying with his grandparents when he learned his parents died hiking in Yosemite Park, a place he can't picture. All he knows is that they never came home.

"Nicky didn't get to see their bodies. The memorial service in lieu of a funeral, to spare him, didn't do him any favors. The service didn't mean anything to a five-year-old boy. Simply speaking, he's bewildered and confused."

"He never talks about Michelle," Rachel murmured.

"He will in time. You've told me she was a superb mother. That's why he won't allow himself to think about her yet. You're his aunt, and close in age to the parents he lost. Having seen pictures, I know you bear a strong resemblance to your brother, as well as to Nicky. The boy relates to you more than he does his grandparents, who are years older and much more sedentary. He's terrified he's going to lose you at sea.

"It's little wonder his dreams have become more violent. He's a year older now. No matter how hard you try to shield him, he's bound to see violence on TV and in films. Nicky's been exposed to more of life, so his demons are worse, and his imagination is running rampant. His mind is wondering about what terrible thing is going to happen to you when you're out of his sight.

"I promise you the truth won't be nearly as hard for him to deal with as his frightening nightmares. He needs closure for something he still can't comprehend. Frankly, you need it, too."

Rachel averted her eyes. Dr. Karsh was right. She'd fought the idea of going to California, for fear she wouldn't be able to handle it. From the beginning he'd urged her to see one of his colleagues who could help her deal with her pain.

Two weeks after she'd learned of her fiancé's infidelity and had called off the wedding, word came that her brother and sister-in-law had died in a freak blizzard on El Capitan in Yosemite. Plunged into the deepest agony of her life, Rachel hadn't listened to a frantic Steven, who'd been unfaithful to her but wanted her back. He'd been trying to reason with her ever since, and vowed he'd wait for her to talk to him no matter how long it took. However, all her energies had gone to Nicky.

When she'd heard the tragic news, she'd been away on a cruise ship, working in her job as an administrator. By the time she'd made it home, their remains had already been flown to Florida. Her whole family had been inconsolable.

Nicky, the poor darling, was still suffering. It was a

miracle he was able to attend kindergarten at all. Rachel had had to go with him every morning and sit in for part of the class in order to reassure him. She didn't dare be late picking him up at the end of his afternoon sessions.

Though she'd purchased a small waterfront condo since graduating college, she'd been forced to sublet it, and move back home with her parents to help take care of her precious nephew. In the past ten months she'd only done six cruises.

They'd coincided with Nicky's vacations from his year-round school. During those times he'd clung to her parents while he waited anxiously for Rachel's return. Not only was it too hard on her mother to nurse her father and care for a five-year-old, but it was asking too much of the cruise line to allow her more time off.

If taking Nicky to Yosemite would help him heal, then Rachel needed to do it, even if it meant opening the wounds all over again. Her nephew simply couldn't go on like this! Neither could she.

Secretly, she harbored a deep anger against the park authorities. The staff in charge were supposed to guarantee tourists' safety. If the right precautions had been exercised, surely such a terrible tragedy couldn't have taken place.

It had been Ben and Michelle's first trip to California. They'd never hiked in mountains like those and shouldn't have done so without supervision. The rangers were there for the tourists' protection. Rachel wondered how lax they would be while she and Nicky visited the area.

Had the ranger in charge at the time been removed? When she was in California, she intended to find out. If she learned he was still working there, she would demand to know why. Depending on the answer, she might start an inquiry to get him dismissed. It wouldn't bring Nicky's parents back, but might prevent another ghastly death from occurring.

"I'm going to take your advice," Rachel said at last. "Nicky's out of school right now, so this would be the best time to go."

The doctor looked pleased. "I can't guarantee the trip will be a total cure, but it's certainly a step in the right direction. Call me when you get back and we'll talk again."

"I will." She got to her feet. "Thank you, Dr. Karsh. I'll let myself out."

After reaching her car, she phoned her boss. Fortunately, he was in his office, and took the opportunity to explain her situation, something she should have done months ago. Not only would she be missing the next cruise, she also gave her two weeks' notice. Nicky's mental health was in jeopardy. She had to put him first, even if it meant looking for another career.

Her boss didn't like it, but said he understood. Would she consider an office job that kept her in Miami? he asked. When Rachel reminded him of her broken engagement to a man who worked in the cruise line's main office, that idea was taken off the table. Before she hung up, she promised to come in the following Tuesday and hand in her formal resignation.

With that decision made, she felt a gigantic weight lift from her shoulders. Of course, she had the daunting prospect of finding a new career, but she'd deal with that after she and Nicky returned from California.

Twenty minutes later she pulled in the driveway of her parents' ranch-style home in Caseil Heights, where she and Ben had grown up. The guest bedroom in the modest Miami house had been redecorated for Nicky. Rachel had painted it blue and white, and found curtains and a bedcover with his favorite Power Ranger and Spiderman motifs.

Before she reached the front door, he came flying out of the house and lunged for her. She'd learned to be prepared, so Nicky wouldn't knock her down. The blond boy was a little taller than average, with a square-shouldered build and strong legs.

Others might accuse Rachel of being biased, but she thought he was the most beautiful child she'd ever seen. Many people agreed with her. Stand him next to the statue of Michelangelo's *David* in Florence, and you would think the sculptor had created David as he might have appeared as a child, curly hair included. If only this trip would help calm Nicky's heart, so he could face life like the young David who slew Goliath, Rachel thought.

"How come I couldn't go with you today?" he asked as they entered the house.

She had to think fast. "Because I've been planning a surprise."

He stared up at her with those solemn, gray-green eyes. "What kind of surprise?"

"Come with me and I'll tell you."

From the foyer she could see through the dining room to the back patio, where her parents usually spent their mornings gardening. Her father's bad heart caused him to tire easily. He would pull a few weeds, then have to get back on the lounger. Her mother did the rest.

One of these days there would be new surgical methods to fix his arrhythmia, but for now he had to be medicated.

Rachel called through the screen to tell them she was back. They knew she'd been to see the doctor, so didn't ask questions in front of Nicky. "We'll join you in a few minutes," she added.

"Take your time," her dad said, eyeing her anxiously. She would have to satisfy him when they were alone.

But first things first. Taking a calming breath, she walked Nicky down the hall to his room. He'd made his bed the best he could, and they both sat down on it. "What's the surprise?" he asked eagerly.

She reached for his hand. "I've been making plans. You and I are going to go on a trip, hopefully tomorrow."

Nicky blinked. "Where?"

Her pulse sped up. "To California."

A long pause ensued. "Where Mommy and Daddy died?"

"Yes." Praying for inspiration, she said, "I want to talk to one of the park rangers and see where your Mommy and Daddy went hiking in Yosemite."

He slid off the bed. "So do I!"

"You do?" Rachel was stunned by his ready acceptance.

"Yes, but are you scared?"

Oh, Nicky… "Scared of what, darling?"

His lower lip quivered. "That we'll die, too?"

She shook her head and hugged him to her. "Of course not. No accident's going to happen to us. I promise."

He pulled away from her. "Then how come we didn't go there sooner?"

Rachel couldn't see him through the blur of tears. Dr. Karsh was a genius. From the beginning he'd urged her to consider the idea, and had warned her to be honest with her nephew no matter how difficult it might be for her. In some ways, her fear appeared to be worse than Nicky's.

"Truthfully, I've been so sad I didn't think I could do it until now."

"Because you loved my daddy and mommy so much, too?"

Out of the mouths of babes. "Yes, darling. That's it exactly."

"Papa and Nana won't be able to come."

"No." She wiped her eyes. "While we're gone, they'll have to stay here. Is that okay with you?"

"I want them to stay. Papa's too tired to walk around."

"You're right." She tousled his curls. "I have to ask you an important question. Since you've never been on a plane before, would you like to fly there? If not, we can take the train, or we can drive in my car. You decide."

"Will it be a jet?"

"Yes."

"Then that's what I want to do. How long are we going to be gone?"

She bit her lip. "I'm not sure yet. Why? Are you worried about it?"

"No. I want us to be gone a long time so you won't have to go on another cruise."

Of course. "I know you don't like my job."

"Why do you have to work?"

"To earn money. Everyone has to earn money to live."

He dropped his head. "I wish you could stay home with me all the time."

"Guess what? After we get back from Yosemite, I'm going to get a job around here."

"What kind of a job?"

"I don't know yet."

"But you won't be going on a ship anymore?"

"Nope. I plan to work as close to you and Papa and Nana as possible."

Nicky lunged for her again, and hugged her so hard it was a good thing she was sitting on the bed.

"Come on," she said with a laugh. "Let's go to my room and make reservations."

He shot out the door ahead of her, to the bedroom she'd had as a girl. Since moving back home, Rachel had transformed half of it into an office, and she now sat down at her computer. After getting her credit card from her wallet, she pulled up the Yosemite Park Web site.

Nicky leaned against her left arm. Luckily, she was right-handed. "What does it say?"

"Yosemite National Park takes up twelve hundred square miles of scenic wildlands. It was set aside in 1890 to preserve a portion of the Sierra Nevada Mountains, in eastern California. The park rises from two thousand to more than thirteen thousand feet above sea level."

"Thirteen thousand?" he cried, his young mind trying to imagine the immensity.

Living at sea level, Rachel was pretty amazed herself. "This says the park has an alpine wilderness, three groves of giant sequoia trees and many impressive waterfalls, cliffs and unusual rock formations."

The headquarters and several hotels were located in Yosemite Village. Probably the best way to get there was to fly to Merced, California, she decided, checking airline schedules. Dozens of early morning flights left daily from Miami, and while Nicky rested against her shoulder, she checked for availability. "Okay. We're booked for a flight to Charlotte in the morning. From there we'll fly to Las Vegas and then Merced."

"I thought we were going to Yosemite."

"We are. From the Merced airport we'll drive into the park." Depending on the summer crowds, the trick would be to find accommodations somewhere in the Yosemite Valley. Tomorrow was Tuesday. Maybe they'd get lucky, and a room would be available before the crush of weekend visitors.

After learning the Ahwahnee Hotel was booked solid, Rachel tried the Yosemite Lodge. "We're in luck, Nicky. There's a room available for Tuesday and Wednesday nights."

"We're only going to stay two nights?"

"No, darling. But June brings so many tourists, we can only stay at the Yosemite Lodge for two nights. After that we'll have to find someplace else. This says the lodge is near Yosemite Falls. See that picture?"

He peered at the screen. "Whoa! That looks like the one in my Tarzan movie."

Whoa was right, except that the cartoon didn't do a real waterfall justice. She hadn't heard him sound this animated since before Ben and Michelle had died.

"Do you want to press this button?"

He nodded and followed through. Soon the confirmation appeared.

"This says we're booked at the hotel for the ninth and tenth. All we need now is a rental car." Another couple of minutes and she'd arranged for one from the airport. "While you tell Nana and Papa our plans, I'll get the suitcases. We need to start packing!"

VANCE WAS ON THE PHONE with Superintendent Noyes when his secretary, Beth, came into the office and put a message on his desk. After glancing at it he whispered,

"Send them in." The middle-aged brunette nodded before disappearing.

Chief Sam Dick and his wife, Ida, didn't need an appointment. As far as Vance was concerned, they topped the park's list of VIPs and were always welcome. He'd been an adolescent when Sam had shown him a secret trail that led from the Yosemite Valley to the Hetch Hetchy Valley to the northwest, where Sam's ancestors had gathered acorns. The chief had provided part of the magic that made up Vance's childhood.

In a minute the elderly Paiute couple stood in the doorway. Vance motioned them inside and told the superintendent he would have to call him back. Once he'd hung up, he walked around his desk and shook their hands.

"This is an honor, Chief. Please, sit down."

"Thank you, Chief," Sam replied, with a glimmer of a smile. It was a joke between them. Vance chuckled, because his own title was only a few years old and would end if, heaven forbid, he got transferred somewhere else. Hopefully, the gods were kind, and Yosemite would be where he worked and lived out the rest of his life.

Vance had grown up using the park as his backyard. It represented home to him, but it had been home to Chief Sam much longer. He came by his title through generations of Mono Paiutes who'd inhabited Yosemite long before the Europeans showed up.

The two gray-haired visitors settled in chairs arranged in front of Vance's desk. Then Sam handed over a large brown envelope. "Take a look."

Vance went back to his swivel chair and examined the two photographs he pulled from the envelope— identical photos. They were copies of a historic picture of a Yosemite Paiute camp taken by the British photographer Edward Muybridge.

"Look at the copy with the number one on the back. That photograph is in the Bancroft Library," Sam told him. "Now look at copy two. It's in the Yosemite Research Library, but notice that the title 'Paiute Chief's Lodge' is missing."

Upon close inspection Vance could see he was right. "Someone etched in the title 'Miwok Lodge' instead." Sam's dark, solemn eyes studied Vance. "Some major funny business is going on at Yosemite National Park. Why was the Paiute title removed? Can you tell me that? There were no Miwoks among my people in this valley. So now you understand why we Paiutes do not have any faith in the park service. I think someone is trying to help the Southern Sierra Miwoks get federal recognition. What are you going to do about this problem, Chief?"

This was no longer a social visit. Sam had come to him as one chief comes to another. In the historical sense it *was* a great honor. Yet in the modern world, Vance feared this was the tip of an enormous political iceberg involving the complex relationship between the Paiutes and Miwoks. Anthropologists claimed both tribes had a shared history in the park going back thirteen thousand years.

"I'm a descendent of the Yosemite Indian and know something," Sam declared. "The park service should listen to us instead of discrediting us. After all, who should know the history better than we do? A bunch of non-Indians who read books written by other non-Indians and their employees who are interested in acquiring a casino?"

Vance understood his frustration. "I feel your pain, Sam." After taking a deep breath he said, "Give me some time. I have no idea who tampered with this photograph. But I swear I'll find out what's going on and—"

The ringing of the phone cut him off. Beth wouldn't have interrupted him if it wasn't an emergency. He put up his hand to indicate he needed to answer it. "Chief Rossiter speaking."

"Vance?" Chase blurted without preamble. "The park has two visitors you need to know about." Along with other duties, Chase was in charge of the bureau of information. Nothing happened he didn't know about first.

Vance frowned. "Has someone from D.C. flown in under the radar?"

"Nothing like that," his friend muttered. "A Rachel Darrow just signed in for a tour."

Darrow? The mere mention of the name was like a powerful blow to the gut. Vance gripped the phone harder.

"She's planning to hike the Mirror Lake loop. I've already alerted security. Sims is running a background check on her as we speak."

Together with Mark Sims, Vance had raised the level of homeland security within the park boundaries. Mounted cameras took pictures of every vehicle and license plate. No one who entered was allowed to pass through without indicating travel plans, home address, a contact person with phone number, and expected length of stay.

"Where's she from?"

"Florida."

Vance broke out in a cold sweat. "Then this is no coincidence."

"I'm afraid not." Chase's voice grated. "She has a young boy with her."

Vance leaped from the chair. "How old is he?"

"I'd say he's at least five, maybe six. I'm as shocked as you are."

"Where are they right now?"

"Outside with some other tourists waiting for Bob, who's about to come on duty to take the group on tour. Naturally, I'm not letting her go anywhere, but she doesn't know that yet. How do you want to handle this?"

Vance's thoughts were reeling. "Tell her I've been informed she's here and I'd like her to come to my office before she does anything else."

"I'll bring her myself. We'll be there in a few minutes."

When Vance hung up, he turned his attention to Ida and Sam, who'd gotten to their feet. The chief's wise old eyes stared at him in that mysterious way they sometimes did when he was seeing a vision.

"After ten springs, we found three fledgling gray owls near the edge of the meadow yesterday," the old man said. "A big change is coming for you."

Ida nodded.

Vance knew the part of the Tuolumne Meadows he was talking about like the back of his hand. To learn that the endangered great gray owl had once again nested there was big news for the park. But the pronouncement coming on the heels of Chase's phone call raised the hairs on the back of Vance's neck. The old man's prophecies had a way of coming true. Vance couldn't bear the thought of his time at the park being threatened in some way. But now wasn't the time to try to figure out what he meant.

Thrown by the revelations of the past few minutes, he said, "Let me keep these photos, and I'll get back to you about this problem as soon as I can."

"Good. See you around, Chief."

Vance walked them out of his office and stopped at Beth's desk. "Chase is bringing a couple of important visitors to my office any minute now. Unless there's an emergency, I prefer not to be disturbed while they're here."

"Understood."

"Thanks."

He went back into his office and returned the superintendent's call, so they could set up another phone conference. Right now Vance's thoughts were far removed from developing strategies that would attract more minorities, specifically African-Americans, to the park. They could examine the Vail agenda for a perspective on the National Parks Service goals another time. After arranging to talk again on Friday morning, Vance hung up the phone.

As he lifted his head, the door opened to reveal a striking blonde of medium height standing in the entry. "Chief Rossiter?" He rose to his feet. "I'm Rachel Darrow. Your secretary said I should come right in," she explained, in a slightly husky voice he found curiously appealing.

"Please," he said, walking around his desk to shake her hand. At a glance, he estimated she was in her mid-twenties. The feminine curves of her body did wonders for the pale blue T-shirt and jeans she was wearing. "Ranger Jarvis informed me there's a boy with you."

Unfriendly green eyes set in that classically beautiful face caught him off guard. "Yes," she replied in a clipped voice. "Evidently my last name rang a bell with the ranger. He told me I couldn't go anywhere in the park until I talked to you first."

"That's right."

"Knowing you wanted this meeting to be private, he offered to show my nephew around headquarters."

So she was the victim's sister.... "What's his name?"

"Nicky."

The boy haunting his dreams now had a name. "How old is he?"

"He turned six three weeks ago. Were you the man in charge when my brother and sister-in-law were killed?" she asked point-blank.

Her aggression caught him by surprise. "Yes. To tell you I'm sorry for what happened couldn't begin to convey my feelings."

The woman's gaze didn't flicker. "I won't even try to describe mine. Just tell me one thing. Was their accident preventable?"

Vance felt the pit in his stomach deepen. "Yes," he answered without hesitation.

"In other words, you might be the almighty king of the great outdoors, but your underlings fell asleep on your watch, and two lives were snuffed out as a result."

Vance had to set the record straight. "My underlings had nothing to do with it. I myself could have prevented it."

Ms. Darrow's softly rounded chin hardened. "So you admit culpability."

"Yes. I take full blame."

A look of excruciating pain crossed her features. "You can just stand there and admit it?" Her cry of agony echoed his own tortured soul.

"Yes." He sucked in his breath.

"I work for a cruise line. Aboard ship it's the captain's responsibility to maintain rigid safety regulations. If a disaster like that had happened during his watch, he would have been relieved of his command and never again given a ship to sail."

Little did she know she was preaching to the converted.

"If you've come to the park with the intention of bringing a lawsuit against me for negligence, maybe you should." It would only be what he deserved, Vance decided.

"Maybe I *will*."

In the next instant she wheeled around, white-faced, and flew out of his office, leaving him staggering. It was like the time he'd survived an IED attack and been flown to a hospital in Germany, only in this instance he'd seen the condemning eyes of his enemy before she'd delivered her salvo.

Vance could have gone after her, but it would cause a scene, something he was loath to do for a variety of reasons. In the first place, he needed to cool down before he approached her again. Second, he was a private person who went out of his way to avoid the inevitable gossip that happened among his staff. It was one of the hazards of his job in a closed community like this.

The phone rang, jerking him back to his surroundings. Vance wheeled around to answer it. "Yes?" he blurted with uncharacteristic harshness, given the way he was feeling at the moment.

"Chief? It's Mark. I've got the information Chase asked me to get on the Darrow woman and her nephew. Do you want it now?"

He closed his eyes tightly. "Go ahead."

"She holds a passport that lists her as a single, twenty-eight-year-old female from Miami, Florida. She works for New World Cruise Lines out of the Port of Miami. Last night she checked into the Yosemite Lodge with her nephew, Nicholas Darrow, and has a reservation there tonight. Room 15. She's driving a blue rental car from the Merced airport. Her return flight to Florida is open-ended. Do you need more information?"

"No. That's ample."

"Is she th—"

"Yes." Vance's clipped answer cut him off. Mark had been on duty that terrible day when the Darrows' frozen bodies had been discovered. Their deaths had negatively affected every park ranger, employee and staff member. "She's Ben Darrow's sister," he added quietly.

"That's tough. Anything else I can do to help?"

Vance cleared his throat. "Have her tailed wherever she goes, and keep me informed." He could hear himself and realized he sounded out of control. Hell…he was!

"I've already asked Chase to keep track of her."

Forcing himself to calm down, Vance said, "Good. By the way, I appreciate your getting me that information so fast. Thanks, Mark."

"You're welcome."

No sooner had he hung up than Beth made another appearance. "Mr. Thurman from the forest service is in the conference room with the others, waiting for you. But you don't look so good." Beth had been here long before Vance had taken over the reins. Nothing slipped past her. "Shall I tell him to start the video presentation without you?"

"Yes. I'll be there as soon as I can."

"I've got some painkillers if you need one."

"Thanks, but no." There wasn't a pill invented to cure what was wrong with him right now.

Chapter Two

Shaking as if she were operating a jackhammer, Rachel went out to the foyer in search of Nicky. When she'd entered the chief ranger's office a few minutes ago, she hadn't known what to expect, but it certainly wasn't the man's total admission of guilt. That underlying current of what sounded suspiciously like sorrow—the kind you couldn't put into words—was an act. A brilliant one.

"Rachel?"

She spun around to see her nephew come running up to her. Ranger Jarvis followed on his heels, carrying his hat. Nicky hugged her around the waist before easing away. "Can we go on our hike now?"

Hike?

During that explosive moment in the chief ranger's office, every thought had been driven out of her head but one. The brown-haired ranger standing next to Nicky examined her with a steady eye. He would have to be blind not to notice how much her brief encounter with his boss had upset her. With the adrenaline still surging, she couldn't think.

"I—I've decided we'll walk around the village and visit the Lower Falls first," she stammered, aware she needed to get ahold of herself. Embarrassed by her behavior, she darted the pensive ranger a cursory glance. "Thank you for watching Nicky for me."

"I enjoyed it. Where are you staying?"

"At Yosemite Lodge," Nicky volunteered in all innocence.

"Would you like to meet for dinner in the dining court? I have to eat, and presume you do, too. They serve good hamburgers."

Had this ranger just been ordered to look after Nicky to make him feel special? An olive branch after the fact? Rachel wasn't in the mood for company, but after the favor he'd done her by watching Nicky, she could hardly turn him down.

He was a far cry from the chief ranger, whose bald admission of guilt had knocked the foundations out from under her. Those slits of blue between his black fringed lashes hadn't asked for understanding. The fact that he made no excuses for the senseless tragedy befalling her brother and sister-in-law had unnerved her in ways she couldn't begin to comprehend.

"Thank you, Ranger Jarvis. We'll look for you, but will understand if an emergency comes up."

"Let's hope this evening's a quiet one." His gray eyes traveled from hers to Nicky's. "See you later." The ranger waved his hat, then put it on before striding off.

Nicky looked up at her. "He said that wolf we saw on the highway was a coyote, because wolves don't live in the park."

"I'm glad to hear it," she answered, though her thoughts were still on the fiery exchange in the chief's office. Together she and Nicky left the building.

The rays of a hot sun overhead portended an even

hotter afternoon. She put a hand on Nicky's shoulder. "Let's get going on our walk."

They wove through the crowds of tourists, until he asked, "Are you mad?"

She might have known she couldn't hide her feelings from him. "About what, darling?"

"Why don't you like that ranger?"

You've got the wrong ranger in mind, Nicky. "I'm sorry if I sounded grumpy just now. I didn't mean to. He seemed very nice. The truth is, I'm tired after our long flight and the drive into the park yesterday."

"Do you want to lie down?"

He was so used to his papa being out of breath, the question was automatic. "That's very thoughtful of you to ask, but no. We came here to see everything we could. Shall we go to the grocery store and get a soda on our way to the falls?"

Nicky nodded. "I want root beer."

"That sounds good to me, too."

While they waited in line to pay for their drinks and snacks, it dawned on Rachel that she'd been the one to sabotage her first meeting with the chief ranger. Rather than behave like a mature woman looking for answers, she'd acted like an angry, out-of-control adolescent with a hot fuse. As a result, she'd learned nothing about her brother's death, and had gained an enemy. What a foolish move.

The whole point of coming here was to help Nicky. So far all she'd done was worry her nephew because she'd let the head ranger get beneath her skin. No matter his provocative manner, she should have concentrated on her mission, and not let his blatant confession of culpability sidetrack her.

Since he took full responsibility for the accident, *he* would be the best person to give her the details. After they came back from their walk she would phone head-quarters and make an appointment with him, hopefully for tomorrow morning.

She would apologize for walking out on him, and they would start over. Together she and Nicky would hear the man's explanation. Her nephew could ask all the questions he wanted, and they would arrange for a tour to the top of El Capitan, where the accident had happened. When Nicky was satisfied, they'd check out of the lodge and drive to some other area of the park, to stay overnight and explore.

With her mind made up, she was actually able to enjoy their walk. The shed architecture of the buildings fit in nicely with the rugged beauty of Yosemite Valley. This paradise of glacially carved rock formations and alpine wilderness beneath a brilliant blue sky was so far removed from Florida's flatland, it was hard to believe both existed on the same planet.

By the time they reached the falls, she and Nicky were enveloped in a fine mist. The moisture helped them cool down. In the background, she could hear a ranger talking.

"The falls drop almost a half mile. Between the upper and lower falls, the intermediate cascades churn through a series of pools and cataracts nearly hidden in a narrow gorge. If you'll notice the cliff to the left, it's dark with moss and lichen because it's constantly wet. Climbers call it the Black Wall. The climb is the noisiest in the park," he added, producing smiles of understanding from the crowd.

Before their accident, Ben and Michelle must have

stood here, marveling over the scenery. Tears rose in Rachel's throat to realize something so tragic could have happened to them in a divine place like this.

As her gaze fell on Nicky, who seemed mesmerized by the gigantic waterfall, a surge of intense love for him swept over her. He'd become her whole life. There wasn't anything she wouldn't do for him.

From the moment he'd lost his parents, she'd thought of him as her son. Rachel had already taken steps to adopt him, and one day soon hoped he'd consider calling her Mom. But first they both needed to put the past behind them. That's why they were here.

Later, on their way back to the lodge, they saw a couple of rangers on horseback. That captured Nicky's interest as nothing else could. While he watched them circulating about, she heard her cell phone ring. Checking her caller ID, she saw it was her parents phoning, and clicked on.

"Hi, Mom. How are you? How's Dad?"

"We're fine. More to the point, how's Nicky?"

"He's doing amazingly well, but of course we've only just begun our exploration." That was code to mean they hadn't been up on El Capitan yet. Rachel realized this was especially painful for her parents, because they hadn't been able to travel with her. "I… It's very beautiful here," she added.

"I don't doubt it. Have the rangers been helpful?"

"Yes." As it turned out, it was Rachel's fault she didn't have answers yet.

"That's good. Look, honey, I realize you can't talk. Call us tonight when Nicky's asleep."

"I will."

"Just so you know, Steven came by last night."

She groaned. Obviously, he'd found out she'd decided to quit her job. "It was over a long time ago. He shouldn't still be bothering you."

"What he did to you I find unforgivable, but I have to admit I've never seen a man so sorry and miserable. He says he'll do whatever it takes to get you back."

After a year, Rachel thought he would have given up by now. "Did you tell him where I am?"

"No, only that you'd gone on a trip with Nicky."

"Thanks, Mom. The last thing I need is for him to show up." He was being so persistent it wouldn't surprise her if he did something like that.

"I know. Well, you and Nicky take care. Tell him we love him, and remember that your dad will want to talk to you tonight."

"I promise I'll phone. Bye for now."

"Rachel?" Nicky spoke the second she'd hung up. "Are Nana and Papa okay?"

"Yes. They said to tell you they love you."

"I love them, too. Rachel? Can we go swimming in the outdoor pool before dinner?"

"I think that's a great idea. I'll race you back to the lodge."

Once they reached the room, she would phone and make that appointment with the chief ranger. Then maybe she'd be able to relax.

As soon as the night crew came on duty, Vance left headquarters for his house, which was within walking distance. After a quick shower and shave, he put on a clean uniform and left on foot for Yosemite Lodge.

En route, he rang reception, and asked to be put through to room 15. He let the phone ring a dozen times, but there was no answer. A call to Chase revealed that Ms. Darrow hadn't left the lodge since her return at four that afternoon. Vance checked his watch. It was six-thirty. No doubt she and her nephew were having dinner, probably in the court dining area.

Various employees smiled at him as he made his way through the lodge. Tourists, talking animatedly, filled every table in the dining area. Already the summer crowds exceeded park staff's expectations. Despite the media's dire warnings of a depressed economy, with gas so expensive, Vance couldn't see it reflected in the numbers. The news would keep the superintendent happy and Vance in his job.

His gaze traveled around the room until the fine sheen of Rachel Darrow's hair caught his eye. Each strand of her stylish feather cut looked like real gold filament. During their troubling blowup in his office earlier in the day, Vance had noticed her many female attributes, not the least of which was her hair.

Chase was eating with her and her nephew. Good. It was just as well he'd be around to help temper the potentially volatile situation. Before Vance did anything else, he needed to apologize to Ms. Darrow for their bad start in his office. Since tonight would be her last night at the lodge, this was his best chance to make contact.

Operating on that decision, he walked through the room toward their table, nodding to the dining-room help who recognized him.

The boy was the first to see him coming. He was good-looking like his aunt, and stared intently at Vance's hat. All little kids did that. Vance had done it himself when he was a boy. There was something fascinating about a ranger's uniform. A few kids even grew up wanting to be rangers. Vance had gone through that phase himself, never dreaming it would actually happen one day.

He approached the boy. "Hello, Nicky. Welcome to Yosemite Park."

"Hi! Who are you?"

"My name's Vance."

His hazel eyes lit up with curiosity. "How did you know my name?"

"I'm the man your aunt came to see at headquarters this morning."

The child tilted his curly blond head back, giving Vance a full view of his face. This was the precious boy whose parents had died on his watch. Searing pain assailed him.

"You're the chief ranger, huh."

"That's right."

Nicky's expression grew sober. "Did you know my mommy and daddy?"

Vance glanced at the boy's aunt, who stared at him without saying anything. Tonight he saw more anxiety and pleading than accusation in the green depths of her eyes. He took her silence to mean he had permission to answer her nephew. After glancing at Chase as well, Vance walked around the table and hunkered down in front of Nicky.

"No, I was never introduced, but I looked for them before and after the storm. When I found them, I helped carry them to the helicopter."

"You did?" His lower lip had started to quiver. The sight practically killed Vance.

"Yes."

Nicky slid off the chair. "Were they dead?"

Vance could hardly breathe. "They were."

"How come?"

"Even though they were told to go back down the mountain because a storm was coming, they thought they would have time to explore a little more. But they got too cold."

"Oh…" The heartbreaking response was just a whisper.

"Sometimes that happens when a blizzard is too fierce and a person can't reach shelter in time. They just got tired and went to sleep, but they didn't feel any pain. I'm sorry, son." Running on sheer instinct, Vance drew the boy into his arms and let him sob quietly against his shoulder. At this juncture he didn't know who needed comfort more.

They hugged for a long time. With each compulsive heave of the small warm body, Vance's heart was torn apart a little more. He blinked back his own tears. "I know how you feel. My parents died in a car crash when I was your age."

Nicky lifted his head to reveal a tearstained face. "They did?"

"Yes. I had to go live with my grandparents."

"Me, too."

"Do you love them?"

"A lot. Do yours live in the park with you?"

"No, they're in heaven."

"So are my mommy and daddy."

"They're all in a happy place now. Did you know my grandparents left their house to me? It's right outside the park entrance. Where's your grandparents' house?"

"In Miami. Rachel lives there, too."

"You're lucky to have an aunt who loves you so much."

"I love her. Do you have an aunt?"

"No. I'm the last Rossiter."

He frowned. "What's a Rossiter?"

Vance chuckled. He couldn't remember the last time he'd had an exchange with a child who was this endearing. In truth, he'd never met anyone who got to his heart the way Nicky did. "Rossiter is my last name. What's yours?"

"Darrow."

"Have you ever been to the Florida Everglades National Park?"

"Yes. Rachel took me after her last cruise. It doesn't have mountains."

"But it has alligators and panthers. We don't have those here."

"Not any wolves, either. Ranger Jarvis told me."

"Ranger Jarvis is right. Did he tell you we have black bears?"

"Yes."

"We also have great gray owls. They're very rare."

"You mean like in Harry Potter?"

"Yes, except they're not white, and their wingspan is four and a half feet." He demonstrated the size by spreading his arms.

"Whoa. I wish I could see one."

"Chief Sam Dick saw three young owls the other day."

"I thought *you* were the chief ranger."

"I am. Sam is a Paiute Indian chief who lives in Yosemite with his wife. He was my friend when I was a child."

"Would he tell you where they are?"

"I already know."

Nicky's eyes rounded. The tears had dried for the moment. "You do?"

"Yes."

"Will you show me?"

"How long are you planning to visit Yosemite?" He asked Nicky the question, but now looked to the boy's aunt for the answer.

Their eyes held for an instant. "I—I'm not sure," she said in a gentle voice. The change in her tone from this morning meant a temporary pax had been achieved, at least. Considering the depth of Nicky's suffering, it was something to be grateful for.

Vance slid his gaze back to the boy. "In case your stay is a short one, why don't you come out to the foyer with me? There's a mural of an owl you'll love. Have you finished your hamburger?"

"Most of it. Can I go with him, Rachel?"

"Yes, of course."

Vance got up. "We won't be long."

When he put out his hand, the boy grasped it. That small trusting gesture tugged hard at his emotions. Together they made their way through the tables to the lobby, hand in hand.

There were a lot of fathers in the room with their children. Vance's protective instincts where Nicky was concerned gave him a strong hint of what it would be like to be a dad. Some people glancing at them probably thought they were father and son. Vance liked the feeling more than a little bit. Who wouldn't love a child as cute and smart and tenderhearted as Nicky?

RACHEL'S BACK WAS to the room, so she would have to turn all the way around to watch Nicky walk off with the head ranger—a man who wore a wedding band on his ring finger. If she'd tried to orchestrate the best scenario to help her nephew let go of his fears, she couldn't have come up with anything as masterful as the way Chief Rossiter had handled the unexpected conversation.

Everything had come out naturally. It was as if he knew exactly what was going on in Nicky's psyche, and chose the perfect words to erase the terror of the unknown. His explanation of events tempered with his own admitted losses gave her nephew something else to think about besides his own grief. She had to confess that she suddenly viewed the ranger in a whole new light.

Without attributing any blame, he'd provided Rachel with enough information to understand that Ben and Michelle had been the ones at fault for not heeding the weather warnings. Her brother had always been the type to push the envelope, always viewing himself as invincible. Shame consumed her for the way she'd harbored anger against the park authorities for something that hadn't been their fault.

Dr. Karsh had hinted that a lot of her anger was really directed at Steven, but to her chagrin she hadn't listened. Instead, in her emotionally charged state, she'd stormed the chief ranger's office this morning, and had virtually attacked him without any facts to back up her faulty assumptions.

It took a big man to let her have her say without retaliating. No wonder he was in charge.

"Are you all right?"

Ranger Jarvis... For a minute she'd forgotten she wasn't alone at the table. "Yes. Forgive me. I didn't mean to ignore you. It's just that I've been so worried about Nicky."

"We've all been worried about him."

His comment surprised her. "What do you mean?"

"That was a terrible day for the park. When we learned your brother and sister-in-law had a child at home, everyone grieved, but no one more than the chief."

Rachel's stomach clenched when she thought of the way she'd treated him.

"As he would tell you, the buck stops with him. In the two and half years he's been in charge, there haven't been any deaths due to negligence on the staff's part. He took it particularly hard."

"Something tells me you did, too," she murmured.

The ranger nodded. "I'm the one who put out the alert that a freak storm was on its way. Those in late spring can be the worst. People outside the park died in it, too. We don't get storms like that very often, but when we do, every measure is taken to protect the tourists. The huge drop in temperature meant gale-force winds and snow were imminent. Every climber and hiker had time to get off El Capitan."

She looked down. "My brother would have seen it as a challenging new adventure. He was a great sailor and weathered many a storm at sea."

"I'm afraid hypothermia is the number one enemy here. He probably thought they had time to hike back to Tamarack Flats, where they'd started out, but the cold prevented them."

"I'm sure that when Nicky heard it was the cold that took their lives, and not some gruesome fall, he was better able to handle the news."

"Does it help *you?*" the ranger inquired gently.

She smiled at him. He was nice. "Yes. I've lived longer, so my nightmares over what happened have probably been worse than his."

"Understood."

Suddenly another ranger approached and asked if he could have a word, saying it was urgent.

"Excuse me," Ranger Jarvis said. As they disappeared, she could hear Nicky's voice behind her. Then she felt his hand on her shoulder.

"You have to see the owl! It's huge! Come on. I want to show it to you."

She half turned in her chair. Once again her eyes met the iridescent blue of Chief Rossiter's. Set in such a rugged, hard-boned male face, they were exceptionally beautiful. By their glint, she had no doubt Nicky had charmed and amused him. Her nephew had a way...

"I'm coming, darling." She jotted their room number on their dinner tab and signed it, then followed him and Chief Rossiter through the dining room to the reception area.

Rachel couldn't help but notice people looking at the tall, imposing ranger. Those who knew him nodded. More than one female had her eye on him. His powerful physique would draw any woman's interest and garner respect and probably envy from the men in the room.

She wondered how his wife dealt with rival attention toward her husband. Rachel surmised they had children. It would help explain how he'd been able to talk to Nicky and comfort him with such ease at a crucial moment.

Interrupting her thoughts, Nicky ran over to the large mural inside the foyer doors. "See the owl's eyes? They look like two suns!"

Trust her imaginative nephew to come up with a creative description. "They certainly do. I never thought of an owl as magnificent, but this one is."

"Did you know they are almost *eggsteenkt?* Vance says he'll show me a real one tomorrow while he's out doing park business. Can I go?"

Already Nicky knew the chief ranger's first name and was using it. Within minutes of meeting him and hearing an eyewitness account about his parents' death from his lips, Nicky trusted him. That was pretty amazing for one brief contact.

"I'm afraid we have to check out in the morning. We only have the room for one more night."

"That's not a problem." Ranger Rossiter spoke up. "They always keep a room free for an unexpected visit by a VIP. I can arrange it."

Nicky stared up at him. "What's a VIP?"

"A very important person. That's you." He reached out to ruffle his curls, and Nicky giggled. Rachel hadn't heard a real giggle come out of him in over a year.

The chief's blue eyes settled on her. "I'll tell the staff to move you to your new room when they come to make up yours tomorrow. That is, if your plans will permit you to stay another couple of nights."

"We don't have *any* plans," Nicky volunteered.

"Nicky…" She bent down and whispered, "Of course we do, and that's not for you to decide," she lectured him. What had gotten into him?

"I'm sorry."

The ranger eyed her intently before taking her aside, out of Nicky's hearing. "If it would fit in with your plans, I'd like him to go with me while I work tomorrow. I have to fly to the Tuolomne Meadows in a helicopter. If we get an early start, we might be able to spot those fledgling owls I was telling him about. It's my thinking that if he explores part of the park tomorrow, maybe he'll remember this as a friendlier place after he goes home."

She couldn't fault Chief Rossiter's reasons for wanting to help Nicky. After what Ranger Jarvis had told her about the collective guilt on the part of the staff, it appeared the chief wanted to do something that would make himself feel better, too.

The problem was Nicky. He might want to come back to the hotel an hour after they'd left, interrupting the headman's workday. Then again... She turned to Nicky and told him what the chief had in mind.

He looked as if he were going to explode with excitement.

"We'll have to leave at six in the morning," the ranger explained. "I'll bring breakfast and lunch for us," he added. "We probably won't be back until dinner."

Nicky raised imploring eyes to Rachel. "Can I go? Please?"

The joy in those eyes blinded her. "I agree it sounds very exciting, but that means we need to go to bed early or you'll be too tired."

"I *never* get tired."

Oh, Nicky. He wanted to impress the chief ranger.

"Be sure and bring your camera," Rossiter was saying.

"I will. See you tomorrow."

"I promise to take good care of him," the chief said sotto voce.

After what Ranger Jarvis had told her, Rachel had no doubts on that score. "I know you will," she whispered back. "Thank you." Her eyes smarted. "I think you know what I'm trying to say."

He nodded slowly, then high-fived Nicky. "Later, sport."

"Later," Nicky called after him as the man strode out the front doors of the lodge. No sooner had he disappeared than Ranger Jarvis joined them.

"Guess what?" Nicky turned to him. "I'm going to see some owls with Vance tomorrow!"

The other man smiled. "Well, lucky you. If anyone can spot them, he can." His gaze flicked to Rachel. "So what are you going to do?"

"I'm not sure. In fact, I'm worried it's too big a responsibility for Chief Rossiter."

The ranger cocked his head. "He can handle it. How would you like to go horseback riding in the morning to pass the time?"

Another goodwill gesture? They were all being very kind. "Won't you be on duty?"

"Not until lunch. Have you ever been?"

"No."

"Then you're in for a treat. I'll show you a spot the average tourist doesn't see. Can you leave by eight? We'll be back before lunch."

"That sounds fun, I think."

He chuckled. Once he'd left, Rachel and Nicky started for their room. "You don't sound mad anymore," the boy said.

"I'm glad you noticed."

"I can't wait till tomorrow. I've never been in a helicopter before. Did you know Vance's favorite treat is Kit Kats, too?"

"Really?"

"Yes, and he likes root beer, but he's going to bring

water, too, because he says root beer makes him thirsty. That's funny, huh."

Very funny. The chief ranger probably had several children and knew instinctively how to please them. Nicky seemed happier than he'd been in a year.

Bless you, Dr. Karsh.

Chapter Three

Rachel set the alarm for five-thirty, but the next morning woke half an hour before it went off. As excited as she was that Nicky couldn't wait to go with the chief ranger, she knew her nephew. Since the accident, he'd always been with her or his grandparents. Their longest separation had been the three hours he spent at kindergarten. Even then she or her mother were always there at the start and end of class to help him with his anxiety.

No matter how thrilled he might be at the prospect of flying in a helicopter and finding an owl, a moment might come when he would suddenly want to come back to the lodge. In fact, she could almost guarantee it, and would hate for that to interrupt Chief Rossiter's business.

Part of her still felt it would be wisest for her to go with them, but Ranger Jarvis had dismissed her concerns. Maybe it was because he knew the chief's wife wouldn't condone it. The best decision would be to call it off. However, Rachel might undo the very thing that would build Nicky's confidence, not to mention the fact that he'd have a hard time forgiving her.

When six o'clock rolled around, and she walked a

euphoric Nicky to the entrance of the lodge, she was a nervous wreck. They'd filled his backpack with everything he might want, including his own little camera and extra film. He chose to wear his favorite Ninja Turtle T-shirt and jeans. His boots would be comfy for any hiking they might do. Rachel couldn't think of anything else he'd need.

"Is that his truck?"

"I think so." It looked like the standard government issue she'd seen on the park roads.

Chief Rossiter met them as they came out the doors. In his uniform he looked...wonderful. "Good morning, sport."

"Hi, Vance! I'm ready to go."

'So I see. Right on time! You'd make a great ranger."

"Thanks!"

He opened the passenger door and helped Nicky into the cab with his pack. Before he went around to the driver's side he turned to Rachel and pulled a tiny notepad out of his breast pocket. "Give me your cell phone number in case I need to get in touch with you."

"I was just going to suggest that." After he wrote it down, she said, "If Nicky gets difficult, let me know and I'll talk to him."

He flashed her a searching glance. "I'll keep that in mind, but I don't anticipate any serious problem."

She wanted to believe that. "Do you have children?"

"No." After a tension-filled pause, he said, "Would you rather he didn't come?"

"Not at all," she cried softly. "I trust you completely. It's just that I know you have heavy responsibilities. A child can be unpredictable at the wrong moment."

One corner of his mouth lifted, turning her heart

over. "Considering it's Nicky Darrow we're talking about, I'll risk it," he replied in his calm, deep voice.

"Thank you," she whispered, touched by the sincerity in his tone. "Since dinner last night he's been living for this."

The chief's eyes narrowed on her upturned features. "Would it surprise you that I have, too?"

Clearly, he was a deeply sensitive man who'd been punishing himself for her brother and sister-in-law's deaths. No wonder he wanted to make recompense by helping Nicky. It moved Rachel to tears.

Hardly able to breathe for the flood of unexamined emotions running riot inside her, she stepped toward her nephew, who was half hanging out the open window. "Be sure to mind Chief Rossiter and do everything he says."

"I will."

As she kissed his cheek, the ranger climbed in behind the wheel. They were going to leave. She felt a wrench in her heart.

"I love you, darling, and I'll be right here when you get back."

"I thought you were going to go horseback riding with Ranger Jarvis!"

"I am, but we'll stay close to the village." The engine revved.

"Okay."

Still no evidence of panic. "Have a wonderful time."

"We will. Bye, Rachel." He was positively glowing in anticipation of their outing.

She waved until she couldn't see the truck anymore. Or maybe it was the tears blurring her vision. Talk about separation anxiety! It appeared Rachel had a serious problem with it. Dr. Karsh would have a field day with her if he knew.

Experiencing a new sense of loss foreign to her, she worked off part of her restlessness by taking a walk to the post office. She'd promised to mail the postcard Nicky had written to her parents. The other part of her restlessness she couldn't do anything about.

By the time eight o'clock rolled around, she tried to be excited about her own coming outing, but couldn't hide her angst from Ranger Jarvis. Upon entering the foyer of the lodge, he took one look at her and asked what was wrong. "Don't tell me it's nothing."

"I won't. The truth is, Nicky and I haven't been separated like this before."

"Naturally, you miss him."

"Yes, but it's more than that. Sometime during the morning or afternoon he's going to realize he's with a stranger. I'm afraid he'll fall apart because I'm not there. When Nicky gets like that it's no fun, believe me. Since Chief Rossiter is out doing his work, I would hate it if he had to stop in order to cater to my nephew."

"The chief's a big boy and understands the stakes. He wouldn't have made the offer if he hadn't felt he could handle it."

She kneaded her hands together. "Nevertheless..."

"Nevertheless you want to be on hand in case your worst fear materializes."

Rachel nodded.

"We can go riding tomorrow and take Nicky with us. How does that sound?"

"Terrific." She drew in a deep breath. "You're a very understanding man."

"A ranger's job is to oblige. Have you eaten yet?"

"No. I couldn't before, but now I'm hungry."

"Then let's go in the dining room. In case the chief sends out an SOS, you'll be here to take care of it."

His suggestion lightened her mood. After a leisurely breakfast, their conversation about the park attractions turned to a more personal nature.

He sipped a second cup of coffee, staring at her over the rim. "What happens when you go back to Florida?"

"I'm looking for a new job. Before we flew out, I quit my old one, to be close to Nicky."

"Is there someone special in your life?"

"Besides Nicky?"

He nodded.

"There was, but I broke off our engagement."

"How long ago?"

"A year."

"Was this before or after you lost your brother?"

"Two weeks before."

"What a horrendous time for you."

"It was." She eyed him curiously. "What about you?"

He didn't pretend not to understand. "I've been divorced going on three years."

"I'm sorry it didn't work out."

"For a long time I was, too, but then you move on."

She sensed he'd been deeply hurt. Maybe she could tell because she'd so recently been through a betrayal herself.

"That's what I'm trying to do, but Steven won't accept it."

"And on some level that pleases you?"

The man had razor-sharp instincts. "I think you were a psychiatrist in a former life."

"Maybe I should have been one so I could have dodged what was coming down the road toward me."

"No. Nicky's psychiatrist would tell you it doesn't work that way." Rachel groaned. "Pathetic, isn't it? He was unfaithful and I don't want him, but…"

"But dreams die hard," Chase stated. "I've been there."

"I suppose it feeds my vanity that he keeps insisting his infidelity was a mistake and he wants me back. Emotionally, I haven't been able to deal with it, not with Nicky's problems at the forefront."

The ranger put down his empty cup and folded his arms on the table. Leaning toward her, he said, "I take it that's why you're here."

"Yes. The doctor said he needs closure."

"Don't we all," Chase murmured sympathetically.

She eyed him frankly. "I'm only now beginning to realize my brother and sister-in-law's deaths affected a whole range of people besides Nicky and me." She lowered her head. "In my pain I lashed out at Chief Rossiter yesterday, without knowing the facts. It makes me ashamed now. I was cruel and he didn't deserve it. When I saw how wonderful he was with Nicky last night and this morning, I'm really embarrassed for my behavior. He's a wonderful man." Her voice was quavering a bit.

There was a slight pause before the ranger said, "You probably didn't say anything to him he hasn't already said to himself a hundred times over. Tell me something. How do you think your brother would have reacted if the chief had ordered him off El Capitan at gunpoint?"

She lifted her head. "Knowing Ben, he would have felt no one had the right to tell him anything. In the heat of the moment he would probably have wanted to throw a few punches first."

Her companion nodded. "Chief Rossiter would have

taken him on, but it's against park policy. Since the accident, that's what has been eating him alive. Next time a situation like this arises, he'll take the law into his own hands to protect a headstrong tourist, even if it means Vance's badge."

"And you'll be there to back him up, right?"

He flashed a smile. "Dead right."

"Ben was a fool."

"Have you ever considered it was their time to go?"

"Yes. It's the only thing that has helped me get through this. But maybe I should start a grassroots movement to change park policy. Chief Rossiter shouldn't have been left to suffer like this over something he couldn't prevent."

"Whether you're serious or not, what do you say we talk about it while we walk the loop you were going to take yesterday?" He got out of his chair. "The wildflowers are out. It's nearby and takes less than an hour."

She rose to her feet. "I'd like that. It's clear I need something to get my mind off Nicky until he's back. Chief Rossiter is too important a man to have gone to all this trouble for him today."

"He wanted to."

"That's what he told me."

"Then believe it and try to enjoy yourself."

She laughed. "I'm sorry. I didn't mean to unload my worries on you."

"That's what I'm here for."

"You're very nice."

AT NOON RACHEL PARTED company with Ranger Jarvis, who'd asked her to call him Chase. They made firm plans to go horseback riding the next day with Nicky. The man had been easy to talk to. The horseback ride would round out their visit before she and Nicky flew back home.

After she got back to her room, she started getting things ready to move to the new room. It turned out to be a suite with more amenities. Nicky would love the little kitchen and the jetted tub.

She sank down on one of the queen-size beds and phoned the airline to arrange for their return flight to Miami. With that done she tried out the tub in the hope of relaxing for a while.

Three o'clock came and went without a call from the head ranger telling her a frantic Nicky wanted to talk to her. Rachel could have phoned her parents, but decided to keep the line free, just in case.

The TV provided background noise. She tried to concentrate on a couple of shows, but couldn't get into them. When six o'clock rolled around without incident, she realized she'd been an idiot to worry. However, by quarter to seven, with no word, she was starting to get nervous for an entirely different reason.

In the middle of her pacing, her cell phone rang. She grabbed for it. "Hello?"

"Ms. Darrow? It's Chief Rossiter."

"Oh—I'm so glad to hear from you!"

"We got back here as soon as we could. Is it all right if I bring Nicky up to your new room? We're in the lobby."

"Of course."

"See you in a minute."

With pounding heart she hurried into the hall to wait for them. They weren't long in coming. The moment Nicky saw her he cried her name and came flying down the corridor. She swept him into her arms. "How was your trip?"

"We had the best time ever!"

"I second the motion," the chief declared in that low, masculine voice.

Over Nicky's blond head her eyes made contact with his. This was the first time she'd seen him without his hat. He was holding Nicky's backpack. His short-cropped hair was black as a raven's wing, adding a potent virility to the total male picture, which was quite stunning.

Embarrassed to be caught staring at him, she buried her face in her nephew's curls. "Did you find those owls?"

Nicky eased out of her arms. "No. We looked and looked, but we couldn't see them anywhere. Vance says we'll have to camp out on Saturday night and watch them when they're moving around in the dark."

Her nephew didn't know it yet, but this afternoon she'd booked their flight to Miami for early Sunday morning. That meant spending Saturday night in Merced. Nicky wouldn't like it, but she would discuss all the details with him after Chief Rossiter went home.

"What was it like being in a helicopter?"

"I *loved* it! You can see *everything!* We spotted bears and deers and elks!"

"Did you take pictures?"

"A whole bunch."

"I can't wait to see them. I bet you're ready for dinner."

"Yup. Vance says he's hungry enough to eat a horse."

Rachel laughed.

"You said we could call the restaurant and have pizza sent up tonight. Can Vance stay and have some with us? That's his favorite food, too, but he likes green peppers and mushrooms and I don't."

Uh-oh. "I have a better idea. Maybe we could invite him and his wife to have lunch with us tomorrow instead. It will be our way of thanking him for giving you a wonderful day to remember."

"But Katy died in the war," Nicky explained. "He's all alone."

Katy? Upon that revelation she shot the chief ranger a pained glance. "I'm so sorry. I didn't know." When she'd asked him if he had children, he'd said no without giving her any other information.

"How could you?" he inquired with enviable calm. Whatever his reasons for still wearing his wedding ring, they were private and had nothing to do with her. But her heart reacted, anyway.

"Can I order it?" Nicky asked before he flew into the room. A second later she could hear his whoops of excitement. "Hey, Vance—come and look at this tub! I'm going to take a bath!"

The headman's lips twitched, adding to his appeal.

She shook her head. "You've been putting up with that kind of enthusiasm all day long. I'm sure you could do with a rest."

"On the contrary. Why don't you deal with his bath while I phone downstairs and order dinner for us. Nicky told me your preferences. He's been counting on this," he added in a hushed voice, to let her know it was her nephew's idea.

Making a split-second decision, because she didn't want the chief to leave yet, she said, "Then let's not disappoint him. Come in."

He followed her into the suite and put the backpack on the nearest bed. She pulled clean pajamas from the dresser drawer and headed for the bathroom. Out of the corner of her eye she saw him pick up the house phone receiver. After taking the whole day off to be with Nicky, no doubt he was ravenous, and had a ton of messages to deal with besides.

Nicky had already turned on the water and was soaping himself. "Where's Vance?"

"He's ordering our dinner. Come on. I'll wash your hair. You've got little pieces of grass and sticks in it."

"We had to crawl around under the trees on our tummies. He let me use his binoculars. They're really, really powerful. You can see an eagle's beak up close from miles away."

"You saw an eagle?"

"Yup. A *golden* eagle. Vance said we were really lucky. It was huge and it had gold feathers on the back of its head. He said the bald eagles usually leave after winter."

"How fabulous for you!"

"Yup. We ate peanut butter and jelly sandwiches and potato chips. I can't wait to go with him on Saturday."

There he went again. But Rachel didn't want to ruin this day for him by talking about going home. Tomorrow morning would be soon enough, after he'd had a good night's sleep.

"I can tell you had a great time."

"Yup. Vance is funny. He taught me a song his grandpa used to sing to him."

Rachel was fascinated by the change in Nicky. She had the chief ranger to thank for infusing her nephew with new confidence. "Can you remember it?"

"I can only sing the first part." He puffed out his lips and made his voice sound gruff. "Oh, I live under the viaduct, down by the vinegar verks, but I'm not like those other jerks 'cause, 'cause…" Nicky stopped singing. "I don't remember any more."

Rachel couldn't help laughing over his excellent imitation. "Maybe it's good you don't," she teased. The for-bidding headman had a rascal side to him. His impact on Nicky was pretty profound. Twelve hours in his company and her nephew still wanted more.

"Okay. Out you come." She turned the handle to let the water drain, and handed him a big fluffy towel. With a hand towel she dried his hair. Soon he was sweet smelling and dressed in his favorite pajamas, printed with cars, eager to rejoin the man in the next room.

When they emerged from the bathroom she noticed the chief was still on the phone. Taking advantage of the moment, she opened Nicky's backpack so he could clean out the papers from his candy bars. She found some lip balm.

"Vance gave that to me so my lips wouldn't burn. It tastes like cherries."

"That was very thoughtful of him." The second the words came out of her mouth, they heard a rap on the door.

"I'll get it!"

"No, Nicky!" She walked to the entry and opened it. A waiter from the dining room stood in the hall, wheeling a cart. "Hello. Come in," she told him.

While the college-age guy moved inside, she searched for her purse to give him a tip, but Vance had already gotten off the phone. "I'll take care of it."

He pulled a bill out of his wallet and handed it to the waiter, who obviously recognized him. A wide smile broke out on his face. "Thanks, Chief," he murmured before leaving the room.

Nicky's head tipped back so he could look up at him. "You know everybody, huh."

The ranger put his strong, suntanned hands on Nicky's shoulders. "You have to when you're in charge."

Rachel moaned inwardly, remembering yet again that he'd been in charge when Nicky's parents had died. What a terrible time that had been for him.

Nicky's earnest hazel eyes stared hard at him. "I want to be like you someday."

Her breath caught while she waited for the ranger's response.

"I have no doubts that when you grow up, you'll be a fine man like your daddy."

"But he wasn't a park ranger."

"A businessman is important, too. I'm sure the people who knew him thought he was the greatest."

"Yup."

"Do you know what, sport? I can smell pizza with sausage."

"Me, too!" Nicky cried. The serious moment had passed.

Rachel transferred everything to the table and the three of them sat down. Normally Nicky could only eat two pieces without the crusts, but tonight he managed three. While they shared a medium pizza, their guest displayed a healthy appetite, consuming his own large pizza and salad without help.

"Vance? Do lady rangers make money?"

"They make money just like the men. Why do you ask?"

"Rachel needs to make mon—"

"Nicky!" she said crossly.

"Sorry."

The chief cast her a speculative glance. "I thought you worked for a cruise line."

"Not anymore," she said. "As soon as we get home, I'm going to look for a job so we can be together."

To her relief their guest began posing questions about Nicky's friends and his kindergarten class.

"What's your teacher's name again?"

"Mr. Plot."

The chief grinned. "That's what I thought you said."

"He has a ponytail," Rachel interjected.

"Yeah. Blake's mommy doesn't like him. She made Blake go in Mrs. Chandler's class."

"Is Mr. Plot a good teacher?"

Nicky nodded. "He's been reading us *The Dumb Bunnies*."

"Are they really dumb?" their guest inquired.

"Yup. They go swimming in their snowsuits and color Easter eggs for Christmas."

"Sounds like a crazy house."

"It is. I'll get it." He slid off the chair and ran over to the dresser. "Here. Rachel bought it for me. Do you want to read it?"

Chief Rossiter nodded his dark head. By the time Nicky pointed out all the funny things on the cover, the ranger was chuckling. Once he started reading aloud, Rachel listened for the moment when he would burst into laughter. She didn't have to wait long. It was impossible to read the silly story without breaking down, and he didn't disappoint her. Soon the three of them were laughing so hard Nicky couldn't catch his breath.

Wiping her eyes, Rachel got up from the chair. "All right, young man. It's time for bed. Go brush your teeth, then I'll tuck you in."

"I want Vance to do it."

She frowned at him. "That's enough!"

Her nephew looked suitably chastened.

Their guest darted her a brief glance before looking

at him. "If you do as your aunt says, I'll stay long enough to hear your prayers."

Given that incentive, Nicky dashed into the bathroom. For a little while Rachel had enjoyed herself so much she was disappointed the unexpected interlude had to end. Nicky was a different child.

"Chief Rossiter, before he comes back I need to apologize for the way I reacted in your office yesterday. Please forgive me. I said some unconscionable things and blamed you for something that was my brother's fault. When you told Nicky what happened, I felt so ashamed."

He rubbed the back of his neck. "I'm afraid neither of us were at our best. The guilt I've lived with has made me difficult to be around. Meeting you meant I had to confront my worst nightmare. I was ready for everything you had to throw at me. Too ready, in fact."

She swallowed hard. "Under the circumstances you showed incredible self-control. I was going to make an appointment with you to apologize. Even though your appearance at dinner last evening changed everything, I want you to know I would have carried through."

Their eyes met and held. "I believe you."

Heavens, he was attractive!

"Thank you for your decency and for the way you talked to Nicky. Today has meant everything to him. I'm so grateful." Her voice shook. "He—"

The little person they were talking about bounced into the room, preventing her from saying anything more. "I'm all done!"

Their guest got to his feet. "Which bed is yours?"

Nicky jumped on the one nearest the windows. Rachel turned down the covers while he scrambled to his knees and said his prayers. When she thought he was through blessing everyone he loved he said, "And please bless Vance. He's my best friend. Amen."

Rachel felt those precious words to the depth of her soul and knew the ranger did, too.

"Amen." The man standing on the other side of the bed sounded equally emotional.

Nicky climbed under the covers and pulled them to his chin. "Vance? Can I come and visit you tomorrow?"

"No!" Rachel answered for him. Her nephew's question didn't surprise her. She'd been worrying about the moment when their guest would have to leave. "He has the park to run. Besides, we're going horseback riding with Ranger Jarvis in the morning."

"I don't want to go." There were tears in Nicky's voice.

"We'll talk about it later. Say good-night to Chief Rossiter."

"Good night, Vance. Thanks for showing me the eagle."

"You're welcome. I had more fun than you did." He high-fived him, then pushed the cart into the hall on his way out.

Rachel followed him into the corridor and pulled on the door until it was halfway shut. "Before you leave, there's something I need to explain."

"I'm in no hurry." He stood there with his hands on his hips in a totally male stance. She eyed him frankly.

"On the advice of his psychiatrist, I brought Nicky out here in the hope he'd get answers to the questions filling his mind, thus stopping the nightmares. After Ben and Michelle died, he fell apart." For the next few minutes she described the difficult year Nicky had been through.

With each revelation, the ranger's grimace deepened. "The poor tyke."

"I can tell your explanation has already helped him

start to heal. Knowing his parents weren't in pain has made a huge difference to him. However, before we go back to Florida, the doctor feels he needs to see the actual place where his parents died. He believes visualizing it will put an end to all the other imaginary fears in Nicky's head."

Rossiter's broad chest rose and fell visibly. "His doctor makes amazing sense. Unfortunately, El Capitan isn't a place for children."

"I know. We saw it while we were driving in." The three-thousand-foot vertical rock formation acclaimed by climbers the world over had terrified her just looking at it. "He doesn't know that was the place where the accident happened. My parents and I kept the details from him, but according to Dr. Karsh, it was the wrong thing to do."

She felt the chief's eyes studying her features. "Let me think about it and I'll get in touch with you tomorrow on your cell phone."

"I'd appreciate that." Her mouth had gone dry from inexplicable nervousness. "I know you've been through a lot today. Thank you."

"He was a pure delight the whole time, but don't think he wasn't missing you. Every other word was Rachel this and Rachel that. If I didn't know better, I would think you were his mother. Every orphaned child should be so lucky."

"Thank you," she whispered. "I'm in the process of adopting him. It should be going through soon."

"Then he's doubly blessed. When are you returning to Miami?"

"Sunday morning. We'll spend Saturday night in Merced. Nicky doesn't know that yet. He thinks he's going camping with you. Was that your idea?"

"I told him I'd discuss the rest of your trip with you. If it fit in with your plans, I'd take the three of us camping."

At the thought of being alone with the chief, heat swarmed into her cheeks. "I'm afraid time constraints make it impossible."

"That's a tough lesson we all have to learn at some point."

She nodded. "As you heard in there, he thinks you're even greater than Mr. Plot. You have no idea what a compliment that is."

Vance rubbed the side of his jaw. "Why are you leaving so soon? There are dozens of things to see in the park."

His question thrilled her. "Believe me, I'd love us to spend a summer here. It's paradise, but I have to earn a living." She tucked a lock of hair behind her ear. "My father's not well. I don't like leaving him or my mother too long. Nicky's the bright spot in their lives."

The rangers gaze traveled over her features. "You've forgotten to include yourself."

His comment sent more warmth through her body. "I agree we all need each other."

"Rachel?"

She rolled her eyes at Nicky's command.

A faint smile hovered around Rossiter's compelling male mouth. "Good night, Ms. Darrow."

"Good night."

Chapter Four

Vance stepped into the night air, having lived through a day like no other. He'd never spent an entire day with anyone's child, let alone been given the total responsibility for his care. In twelve hours plus, the orphaned boy, who'd been lurking faceless and phantomlike in the recesses of his mind for the past year, now had features and form.

Nicky Darrow, the sweetest child Vance could ever imagine, had found his way into his heart. The knowledge that the boy had been suffering so severely only fired Vance's determination to do whatever he could to help Nicky find peace while he was here.

His aunt Rachel had just presented Vance with a problem that needed to be solved while she and Nicky were still in the park. Several options came to mind. By the time he'd arrived at his house, he'd thought of a plan. He would arrange it for Saturday morning before they left for Merced.

While Rachel's appealing image lingered in his thoughts, he took off his uniform to shower. Once he'd pulled on the bottom half of a pair of sweats, he listened to his phone messages. With no problems to deal with until tomorrow, he called the pilot who'd flown Vance in the helicopter during the search and rescue mission atop El Capitan last year.

"Perry?"

"What's up, Chief?"

"Sorry to bother you this time of night, but somewhat of an emergency has come up. I'd like to run this by you and get your opinion."

"Go ahead."

In the next few minutes Vance went into detail about the Darrows' situation and his plan. "The boy's psychiatrist feels he needs to see the place where his parents died, and talk to the people who dealt with them, whatever their capacity. Since you were at the controls when we found their bodies, Nicky can get answers only you would be able to provide. Their deaths have crippled him emotionally."

The other man whistled. "The poor kid. Sure, I'll do it. If he were my child, I'd hope he would get every bit of help possible to recover."

"You're a good man," Vance said in a gruff tone. "What's your Saturday morning like?"

"I'm available." Even if he wasn't, Vance knew the former navy pilot had made Nicky his first priority without hesitation. Every park employee felt the same sadness. The Darrows' death would never be forgotten. "If we go up at seven, there'll be less wind."

"We'll be there on the dot. I owe you, Perry."

"You've got that wrong. After what happened to them, I like the idea of doing something for the boy if it'll help *me* sleep better nights."

Vance's eyes closed tightly. "Amen to that. See you Saturday." They clicked off.

He sat on the side of the bed with his head down, his

hands clasped between his legs. Except for emergencies that required him getting around in the helicopter because of the vast distances, Vance didn't allow air traffic of any kind over the park, not even a glider. The noise disturbed natural habitat.

Today he'd broken his own rule by asking one of the guys to fly him and Nicky to the Tuolomne Meadows. He'd do it again to see the way the boy's eyes had lit up at the sight of that eagle.

If the truth were known, he felt a keen disappointment that Nicky's visit to Yosemite with his beautiful aunt was going to be short-lived. It had been years since Vance had known real joy in his life. Today had been one of those rare times. Nicky was a miracle. The boy's prayer still rang in his ears.

And please bless Vance. He's my best friend. Amen.

Too restless to sleep yet, he got up from the bed and wandered into the kitchen for a glass of ice water. He leaned over the sink to look out the window at the sky. It was a beautiful night, but the stars would be even more spectacular seen from the meadow at an elevation of nine thousand feet. Rachel would be enthralled. He'd love to stare into those gorgeous green eyes while she stared into the heavens.

Nicky would love it, too. He absorbed knowledge like a sponge. Vance would have the time of his life showing him the constellations. You never knew what question the kid was going to ask next.

He'd entertained Vance all day, wanting to know things like what made the wind move? Had Vance ever seen a pine tree grow? Why is the eagle bald? How come we have to get old? Why can't I live in the park, too?

The last question gave Vance pause. Nicky had a reverence, as well as an affinity, for the outdoors. He'd learned a lot on his trip into the Everglades and demonstrated it in a number of ways. Most children seeing a nest of eggs in one of the sapling pines would want to reach in and take one, or at least examine it. Not Nicky. Without being told, he hunkered down at a discreet distance and simply waited for the mother chipping sparrow to return.

Vance saw so much of himself in the boy's wonder of nature, it hurt. When Vance had gone into the military, he'd done so because his own father had been a marine and had taught him the importance of serving his country. But Vance had a lot of his grandfather in him, too. The older man's love of the outdoors had rubbed off on him at an early age. With the park right next door, it beat every other destination.

This was home. No matter the outcome of Chief Dick's prophecy, Vance would never leave. On some level he felt an irrational pride in Nicky's love of Yosemite. Considering that the boy's parents had died here, it was pretty astounding.

His aunt's courage was even more astounding. She was older, and learning the facts surrounding her brother and sister-in-law's deaths hurt more, but she'd persevered because of her love for Nicky. Whoever said a mother would walk through fire for her child would have to include Rachel Darrow.

The idea of her leaving so soon filled him with a sense of loss he couldn't fathom. Rachel was an exceptional woman. Knowing how precious her nephew was to her— even to giving up a career to be close to him—she'd still entrusted Nicky's life to Vance for a whole day. It showed a degree of forgiveness and faith that humbled him.

After draining his glass, he headed for bed. He had a big day tomorrow. So did Chase, apparently....

When his friend had escorted her to headquarters, Vance hadn't given it a thought. He hadn't questioned Chase's desire to look after the boy for a little while so Vance could interview her in private. He hadn't been concerned that Chase ate dinner with her and Nicky, because he knew Mark had asked him to keep an eye on her. It was all perfectly understandable.

Until now...

That his best friend was going to enjoy time with her horseback riding in the morning had come as a surprise. For some inexplicable reason the knowledge not only irritated Vance, it disturbed him.

He knew his reaction was as irrational as his behavior had been with her in his office. Trying to get comfortable, he pounded the pillow. It was a free country. Chase had every right to pursue any attractive woman he wanted. In fact, Vance encouraged it. The former navy meteorologist turned ranger was too fine a man to go through life embittered by his divorce, unable to move on with someone else.

Like Vance, was Chase inordinately attracted to Rachel? What man wouldn't be? Or was he trying in his own way to assuage his guilt over what had happened to Nicky's parents?

No matter the answer, it was a moot point, since she'd be leaving in another two days. Hardly enough time for anything to happen.

Except that wasn't true if she felt an attraction to Chase.

Tonight when Vance had said good-night to her in the hall, he hadn't gotten the feeling Chase was on her mind. He'd seen her eyes darken with emotion when

Nicky told him Katy had died in the war. What had been going on in her psyche just then?

He'd give a lot to know. *And then what, Rossiter?*

Depending on the answer, absolutely nothing. He'd lost Katy. No way did Vance want to love someone that deeply again, when he couldn't be guaranteed a happy ending. If Chase was fool enough to get burned a second time, he did so at his own risk.

NICKY HAD BEEN PERFECT until this morning. Rachel looked at the plate of food he hadn't touched since they'd come to the dining room for breakfast.

"Ranger Jarvis will be here in a few minutes. If you don't eat, you won't feel good during our horseback ride."

He leaned back in his chair. "I don't want to go. Maybe Vance will let me sit in his office until you get back. I won't bother him."

"Do you know what, young man? Ranger Jarvis has gone to a lot of trouble for us. He's had to find horses and get everything ready. I don't want to disappoint him. Do you?" she asked pointedly.

His pout was back. "No," he admitted, "but I don't want to go." Here came the tears.

She straightened in the chair. "Sometimes we have to do things we don't want to do."

"How come?"

Rachel couldn't take much more. "Nicholas Darrow, you *know* why. If you're going to behave this way, we'll stay in the room today and won't see anybody. I mean it."

While she waited for him to decide, her cell phone rang. She pulled it out of her purse, but didn't recognize the caller ID. Maybe it was Chase. If he had to cancel their outing because of an emergency, it would solve this morning's crisis. Perhaps that would be for the best.

"Hello?"

"Ms. Darrow? It's Chief Rossiter."

Her pulse raced for no good reason. "Oh, hello!"

"Is it Ranger Jarvis?" Nicky asked. "I hope he can't come."

She frowned at him.

"I hoped to catch you before you left with Ranger Jarvis."

Rachel glanced at the entrance to the dining room. "He hasn't arrived yet. Nicky and I are still eating breakfast."

"Nevertheless, I'll make this quick."

"Is it Vance?" Nicky sat up, looking eager.

"Hush!" At her wit's end, she turned her back on him. "Excuse me. Please, go on."

"I've arranged for a helicopter to fly us to the top of El Capitan tomorrow at seven in the morning. Nicky will be able to see everything firsthand and ask questions of the pilot who was part of the rescue team last year. It won't take more than an hour. Why don't you discuss this with Nicky? If he has a problem with it, call me tonight."

Rachel got to her feet. "There's no problem. He needs all the truth you can supply. We'll be ready."

"Then I'll be by for you at ten to seven."

"Thank you so much."

Nicky had run around in front of her. "Can I talk to him? Please?"

The chief chuckled. "I can hear Nicky. Tell him I want to say hello, too. Go ahead and put him on."

"You have more patience than I do. Just a minute." She handed him the phone. "Say hi, but don't talk long."

"I won't." He put it to his ear. "Hello, Vance? It's me!" The smiley face was back in full force. Whatever they started talking about made Nicky laugh. He'd forgotten all about Rachel.

"Hi," a male voice said beside her. Startled, she turned to discover Chase standing there in his uniform.

"How are you?"

"Good. Is Nicky talking to his grandparents?" he asked in a quiet voice.

She shook her head and moved a few feet away from her nephew. "Chief Rossiter phoned. When Nicky heard who it was, he begged to talk to him." Maybe the exchange would supply the magic needed to put her nephew in a more affable mood.

Chase's expression sobered. "Is everything all right?"

While Nicky was occupied, she took advantage of the time to tell him what the chief had arranged and why. "I'm very grateful and just hope it helps Nicky."

"We all want that."

"I know. Everyone's been terrific."

Afraid Nicky was staying on the phone too long, she tapped him on the shoulder. "You have to hang up now. Chase has come for us."

He frowned. "Okay. Hey, Vance? Rachel says we have to go horseback riding now. See you later, alligator. What? Refrigerator?" He burst into laughter. "See you later, elevator." He handed Rachel the phone with noticeable reluctance.

Chase smiled down at him. "Hi, Nicky. Sounds like you and the chief were having a fun conversation."

"Yup."

"Did you know Daisy's waiting for you?"

He cocked his head. "Who's that?"

"Follow me and you'll find out."

Nicky looked puzzled. "I didn't know a girl was coming with us."

"That's my surprise." He winked at Rachel as he said it. Ranger Jarvis really was a terrific person.

She grasped Nicky's hand. "This is exciting. I want to meet her, too. Let's go."

Rachel had already asked that the tab be put on their room bill. They left the lodge and found his Pathfinder parked close by. Chase helped her into the front seat and opened the back door for Nicky. Soon they were off.

"The stable is a couple of miles from here. Have you ever been horseback riding, Nicky?"

"I've ridden a pony at Blake's birthday party."

"Did you like it?" Chase asked.

"I guess."

"You know you did," Rachel said as she swiveled in her seat.

"Is Blake your best friend?"

"No. Vance is."

The ranger's brows lifted. "You have a friend with the same name as our chief ranger?"

Rachel held her breath, knowing what was coming. "No. The *chief's* my best friend!" He said it in a way that suggested Chase should have known and understood.

"Then you're a lucky boy."

"I know."

Nicky's behavior was an embarrassment. Rachel was relieved when they drew up to the stable. There were several groups of tourists standing around to get outfitted, but Chase walked right past them to a corral where two horses and a pony were waiting.

He grabbed the reins. "Nicky? Meet Daisy."

Her nephew blinked. "You said she was a girl."

"She is. A little filly just the right size for you."

"Vance says I'm a big boy."

"And so you are." He lifted Nicky into the saddle. While he adjusted the stirrups, Rachel climbed on the mare one of the stable hands was holding for her. She was horrified by Nicky's behavior and shot him a warning look.

"Can you thank Chase for helping you? He's gone to a lot of trouble for us."

Nicky lowered his eyes. "Thanks."

"Thank you, Chase," she admonished.

Chase gave a shake of his head, as if to say, *Don't worry about it. I'm a big boy and understand what's going on here.*

Rachel wished *she* did. Yesterday the chief ranger had shown Nicky a wonderful time, but it shouldn't have caused him to spurn Chase's attention. She was really cross with him right now.

Chase climbed on his horse and sidled next to Nicky. After showing him how to hold the reins, he flashed Rachel a glance. "Let's go."

The pony walked next to his horse as he led the way out of the corral. They followed a well-worn trail that passed through a lush meadow bordered by dark forest. It was a glorious morning. Rachel wanted to enjoy it if Nicky would let them.

Their companion was a special man to put himself out for a child who was being obnoxious. She'd never seen her nephew act in such a rude manner. Since he'd spent the day with the headman, a whole new side of Nicky had come out, one she didn't like.

Deciding not to feed into his little tantrum, she caught up to Chase on the other side. For the next half hour they rode at a leisurely pace. Chase pointed out the famous granite landmarks for which Yosemite was noted.

Moved by the beauty of it, Rachel let out a sigh. "The landscape is spectacular."

"Vance climbed all those cliffs with his grandpa!" Nicky announced.

By now she was positively embarrassed. "Really?"

"Hundreds of times!"

"Hundreds?" Chase asked with a poker face.

"Yup. He's done everything! Rachel, can we go back and swim now? I'm tired and thirsty."

Even Chase knew when to quit. He pulled to a stop and handed the boy a bottle of water from his saddle-bag. "Drink it all. It's yours."

Nicky took it from him. "Thanks."

To Rachel's relief her nephew had remembered his manners.

"You're welcome." Chase handed Rachel a bottle and produced another one for himself, which he drained.

She drank most of her water. "That tastes good in this heat. Thank you."

He nodded. "Okay. Let's head back."

"Hooray! Maybe Vance can swim with me after he gets through talking to the super something."

"Superintendent?" Chase suggested.

"Yeah. Who's that?"

"The head of the whole park."

"I thought *Vance* was the head."

"They both are, but the superintendent's not a ranger. He works for the government."

"Does that make him mad?"

Chase eyed Rachel in puzzlement before they both chuckled. "I don't know," he said.

"I bet it does," Nicky declared.

"Why do you think that?" Rachel was curious to understand what was going on in his mind.

"'Cause he's not tough like Vance. Vance was a marine!"

Rachel hadn't known that. No wonder the chief ranger was such a paragon in Nicky's eyes. Her father's bad health throughout his adult life wouldn't allow him to join up, but he thought marines walked on water, and his grandson knew it.

"Vance is the toughest man I know," Chase stated.

"See, Rachel? Ranger Jarvis thinks so, too."

Yes, she saw a lot of things. So did Chase. Chief Rossiter was an impossible act to follow.

When they got back to the lodge, Chase said he'd wait out by the pool for them while they went up to the room. Since he had to go on duty soon, Rachel stayed in her top and jeans. As soon as Nicky put on his suit, they hurried out to the pool, where a lifeguard was on duty.

Chase found them a table by the edge, where Rachel could keep a close eye on Nicky. Lots of kids were in the water. One boy about his age stayed in the shallow end with him, and they started talking. Before coming to the park, Nicky would have hung back. Though alarmed by the way he treated Chase, as if he were expendable, she was pleased to see her nephew coming out of his shell.

"I'm sorry for the way he's been acting, Chase."

He studied her for a moment. "Don't apologize. There's a reason for it and we both know what it is."

She did know. Chase's boss was Nicky's closest connection to the father he'd lost, aside from his grandpa, of course. "I can see that Steven would never get through Nicky's shell, even if we ended up getting married."

"Then you *have* been thinking about your ex-fiancé?"

"Honestly?" She darted him a glance.

"I wouldn't have asked otherwise."

"Not until my mother phoned night before last and told me Steven had been to the house to see me. She said he's really broken up over what he did. Maybe he is. I know there are some couples who manage to work through infidelity issues."

"That's true, but I couldn't."

"Was your ex-wife unfaithful?"

"No. We had other issues that couldn't be resolved." Whatever they were, he wouldn't talk about them, and she wouldn't press.

"Steven had been seeing a woman who played with the ship's band before he started dating me. I fell hard for him. When he proposed, I was thrilled. He works in administration for the cruise line. A month before we were to be married, he went on one of the cruises I didn't, ostensibly to oversee the ship's operation.

"I learned later that he and his former girlfriend got together. He swore it was only to comfort her because they were in a storm one night near Bermuda and thought they might not make it back to shore. He claimed he never meant for things to get out of control, that it would never happen again.

"As one of my colleagues has pointed out, we aren't married yet. Maybe I should give him a second chance. That's easy enough for her to say, but I'm afraid my feelings can't be resurrected."

Chase studied her for a long moment. "But you don't know for sure."

"Nicky's doctor says I need to explore my feelings, because Ben and Michelle's deaths didn't allow me to resolve anything. I'm sure he's right, but now there's another problem."

"Nicky."

She nodded. "When Steven asked me to marry him, neither of us could have imagined a scenario where I would be adopting Nicky. I'm sure instant fatherhood wasn't what he had in mind, unless it was his own child. Even if I decide to try seeing him again, nothing could happen until Nicky really gets to know him and is comfortable with him."

A long silence ensued. "When are you going back?"

"Saturday. I plan to drive us to Merced and stay overnight. Our flight leaves early Sunday morning. I have to be back to see my old boss on Tuesday. If there's a chance that Steven and I can still work things out after a year's separation, then I need to listen to him. At least that's what the doctor advises, otherwise I could have years of regrets and what ifs. I don't want that."

"He's a wise man."

"After Chief Rossiter takes us up on El Capitan, we'll find out if the doctor's counsel worked and Nicky's nightmares end."

"We'll all hope for that," the ranger declared.

"Chase? Thank you for everything you've done. For listening. I won't forget."

His eyes searched hers. "I'm glad you came to the park. It helped all of us, too."

Rachel smiled.

"Good luck in sorting everything out." He rose to his

feet. "No. Don't get up. Nicky's still having fun in the pool. Have a safe flight home."

"Good luck to you, too, Chase."

VANCE WAS FINISHING off the last of his tuna sandwich when his cell phone rang. He reached across the kitchen counter for it, squinting to see who was calling. He clicked on.

"What are you doing, phoning me? Here I've been imagining you on that horseback ride enjoying yourself." Vance had never been jealous of another man and he wasn't going to start now. This was *Chase* he was talking to. His best friend!

Chase chuckled. "Not with Nicky along."

"What's wrong? He didn't get thrown, did he?"

"On Daisy?"

"Then he's all right?"

"Take it easy, Vance. You're beginning to sound like a parent."

Maybe because for the first time in his life he felt like one. Vance took a stabilizing breath. "Let's start this conversation over. What happened today?"

"Let's just say you are Nicky's new hero and let it go at that."

Though the words were gratifying to hear, a scoffing sound escaped his lips. "You know how kids are. It'll pass once he's back in Miami."

"Want to bet? You would have to have lived through this morning to know what I'm talking about. Take it from me. You've got a fan for life."

Though Vance didn't want to ask the next question for fear of the answer, he had to. "How did it go with Rachel?"

"What do you mean?"

He held his breath. "You know exactly what I meant. Do I have to spell it out?"

"If you're saying what I think you're saying, you've got things all wrong. I admit Rachel's a good-looking woman. When I found out who she was and walked her and Nicky over to your office that first morning, I decided I'd like to get to know her better. But when she emerged from your office, I could tell something earth-shaking had gone on in there. She acted like she didn't know what had hit her. I made a few attempts but was never able to get to first base with her.

"When you walked into the dining room that evening, you acted the same way, like you'd been struck by an unknown force. What saddens me is that you've been reeling ever since, without doing anything about it, because you figured I found her first and it was finders, keepers. Right?"

Chase was too smart for his own good.

"Vance, that might have worked when we were little kids, but we're grown men. Today I was just trying to be her friend. Right now she could use one, because she's been in hell for over a year."

For the next few minutes Vance listened to Chase's explanation. "It appears her ex-fiancé wants a second chance. On her psychiatrist's advice, she's going back to Florida with the intention of discovering her true feelings."

That unexpected piece of news knocked Vance sideways, but he refused to examine all the reasons why. "Did she actually *tell* you she wants to get back with him? That's strange, because that wasn't the message I got from Nicky. In fact I can assure you right now he doesn't like Steven and never will."

"Agreed. There's just one man who lights up his world."

"That's only natural," Vance growled. "It all comes down to my not finding his father on El Capitan before it was too late."

"I think we're talking at cross purposes here."

He rubbed his temple, where he could feel a tension headache coming on. "What do you mean?"

"I wasn't referring to his father. It's *you* Nicky's crazy about. I realize his feelings are over the top right now because of his loss, but he has definitely bonded with you."

It worked both ways, but by now Vance's thoughts were churning. Rachel's need to see her ex-fiancé again would explain why she didn't want to stay at the park any longer. Hell. "Where are you now?"

"Back on duty. In case you've finished your business with the superintendent, whose credentials don't include being a marine, tough or otherwise, there's a little guy who's waiting for the chief ranger to show up at the lodge swimming pool and make his day. Talk to you later."

Chase rang off, leaving Vance standing there in shock. The temptation to do as his friend suggested prompted him to phone Beth.

"What's on the docket for this afternoon?"

"You asked me that question an hour ago and I told you there's nothing that can't wait until tomorrow. That's why you went home for lunch, right?"

"Right."

"Barring an earthquake or another forest fire that I don't know about yet, I presume there's still nothing."

He smiled. "Just making sure."

"Chief? Are you okay? You've been acting different since Chief Dick showed up the other day. What did he do? See your future in a ghost dance?"

Vance shivered. She was too close to the mark. "Were you eavesdropping?"

"Who? *Moi?*"

"Come clean now."

"Sorry. That's not part of my job description."

"Beth? Don't ever change." Still chuckling, he said, "Chief Dick will be in next week. Since I never know when he's coming, I might not be in the office, so make a note to tell him I've fixed things at the library. The photograph now says Paiute Lodge. He'll know what I mean. The brown envelope he left me is in my Out basket, marked 'Chief Dick.' Give that to him, too. It should make him happy."

"Will do."

"Now I think I'm going swimming."

"In the middle of your workday? Since when?"

Since Rachel Darrow burst into my world a few days ago. Of course he didn't tell Beth that. "Keep it under wraps, *if* you can."

Hanging up on her protest, he went in search of his plaid swim trunks. After stripping off his uniform, he put them on, then stepped into a pair of jeans and a T-shirt. Once he'd pocketed his phone, he made a detour to the bedroom closet for his snorkel. Now he was ready, and took off for Yosemite Lodge on foot.

A few minutes later he surveyed the crowded pool, looking for Nicky and Rachel, but to his disappointment didn't see them. Maybe they'd gone inside to eat lunch. He'd wait fifteen or twenty minutes before he gave it up and went back to work.

In a quick movement he took off his jeans and shirt and dived into the deep end. With so many bodies in the water, the idea of doing lengthwise laps was out of the question. He would have to be satisfied swimming to the bottom of the pool to stay occupied and anonymous.

Ten minutes passed. More people had entered the pool, including a bunch of college-age guys who began playing water polo, and gave the lifeguard grief by ignoring him. During family hour, games weren't allowed. If they didn't stop in about one minute, Vance was prepared to step in.

The next time he came up for air, he heard wolf whistles. His breath caught when he saw what had produced them. A golden-blond woman with an eye-catching figure and great legs came walking toward the shallow end of the pool. Her modest two-piece turquoise suit matched the trunks of the curly-headed blond boy holding her hand.

"Hey, babe, come and play with us!" one of the guys called to her. He held up the ball, ignoring the lifeguard's whistle.

Primordial instinct took over as Vance shot through the water like a torpedo and snatched the ball away. Quick as lightning he levered himself onto the deck. After tossing the ball to the lifeguard, he turned to the guys, who'd started swearing at him.

"This is family hour, gentlemen. You want to play polo, then come back at eight tonight when no children can be hurt. I'm giving you thirty seconds to disappear."

"Make us," challenged the brashest one.

Vance dived in and put a hammerlock on him. "You can go quietly and I won't press charges, or you can resist arrest and all four of you can tell the federal court judge why you're out of control. It's your call if you're ever allowed to step foot in Yosemite Park again. What's it going to be?"

He tried in vain to break Vance's hold. "Who in the hell do you think you are?"

"Do you really want to find out?"

"Come on, Derek," one of his friends muttered. The three of them climbed over the side and headed for the men's changing room.

When Derek finally stopped struggling, Vance loosened his hold. "Better go with your friends, who had the good sense to leave."

The guy finally got out, but his eyes were glittering with rage. "Better watch your back, tough guy," he threatened before walking away.

While everyone in the pool broke into spontaneous applause and cheers that the menace was gone, Vance swam to the other side. He vaulted to the tile and reached for the phone in his jeans.

"Mark? It's Vance. Send extra security to Yosemite Lodge stat and pick up four college-age guys I've just ejected from the pool. They've been drinking." He gave their descriptions.

"We're on it."

As he hung up, the lifeguard approached him. "Thanks for helping me out, Chief Rossiter. When you took over I thought I was watching a combination of Steven Segal, Bruce Willis and Arnold Schwarzenegger all rolled into one."

The exaggeration amused him. "No problem."

Behind them he heard a female voice cry, "Wait, Nicky, you're not supposed to run!"

"Vance!"

The next thing he knew, a warm, sturdy little body launched into him and grabbed on for dear life. Laughing with pleasure, Vance picked him up. Over Nicky's curls his gaze fused with a pair of eyes the color of new spring grass at the highest elevation in the park.

Vance was exultant to note he saw nothing unfriendly in their depths right now, a far cry from Wednesday morning in his office.

Chapter Five

"Nicky was right about you."

The chief ranger's eyes glowed an intense blue. "In what way?"

"You can take care of yourself and anyone else around. It makes a little boy feel secure."

Rachel would have added that it made her feel safe, too, but he might think such a personal comment meant she was flirting with him, the last thing she intended to convey.

A man who wore his deceased wife's wedding band did it because he never planned to marry again. The wise woman seeing it on his ring finger knew better than to make a fool of herself by assuming she could get him to remove it.

"Come on, Nicky," she urged. "Let's have our swim."

"Why don't we all jump in?" the chief suggested. "Hold your nose, Nicky."

"Okay."

"Ready?"

"Yup!"

All of a sudden the two of them landed in the deep end. It made a huge splash, getting her soaked. Nicky shrieked with laughter. The man holding him tilted his dark head back. "What are you waiting for, Ms. Darrow?"

Her insides fluttered. "Not a thing."

She jumped in next to them, creating enough havoc to delight her nephew and bring a devilish smile to the chief's lips. While she treaded water, he turned Nicky on his back to float, encouraging him to kick hard. Rachel had taught her nephew the fundamentals of swimming. Under his hero's watchful eye now, Nicky showed amazing progress. That was because he was having the time of his life.

At one point the chief reached for his snorkel lying on the deck. It provided more entertainment for Nicky. Time flew by. In the process of having fun, her nephew ignored the hot sun shining down. Though Rachel had put sunscreen on him, those tender shoulders were being exposed too long.

"I hate to break this up, but it's time to go in, darling. Otherwise you'll turn into a lobster."

"But I don't want to get out!" He sounded so upset she felt like the wicked witch for ruining his fun.

"Okay. That's it!" She grabbed his hand with the intention of going up to the room, but was forestalled by their companion putting Nicky on his shoulders, distracting him. Vance's gaze found Rachel's. Whenever he looked at her in that direct manner, her senses quickened.

"Your aunt's right, Nicky. Dive off one more time, then we'll get changed and go over to headquarters. I think a root beer is waiting for you."

Nicky shot her a pleading glance. "Can I?"

She didn't like rewarding him for bad behavior, but since it was the chief ranger's suggestion, she relented. "Maybe for a little while."

"Hooray!" Nicky complied at once and got up carefully, standing on Vance's broad, sun-bronzed shoulders. Slowly he let go of his hands. "Okay. I'm ready. Watch me, Rachel!"

He executed a perfect little dive. When he emerged, she smiled and clapped. "You two make quite a team."

"You think?" The chief sounded pleased. He swung Nicky onto the deck and then levered himself from the water with effortless male grace. Rachel swam over to the ladder and climbed out. He studied her as she walked toward them. Delight filled her, a reaction she couldn't control.

"Will ten minutes give you and Nicky time to shower and change?"

Rachel nodded. "I'll bring him down to the lobby."

"Good." Glancing at Nicky, he said, "See you later, Terminator." After giving him a high five, he gathered his things.

"See you later, operator!" Nicky called back unexpectedly. The clever boy was determined to keep up with him.

That brought a happy bark of laughter from the chief before he headed for the men's changing room. His hard-muscled body turned female heads left and right, including Rachel's.

She grasped Nicky's hand and they left the pool area for their room. He chatted the whole way about his favorite person, and continued nonstop throughout his bath. She showered quickly, then they both dressed before she accompanied him to the lobby.

Nicky ran up to the head ranger, who was now wearing jeans and a white T-shirt. As she'd discovered at the pool, the man didn't need a uniform to make him stand out. On the contrary...

"Wait, Nicky!" She held him back because the chief was talking on his cell phone, but he didn't keep them waiting long.

"What's in your pocket, sport?"

"Timberwolf."

"When we get to my office, you'll have to show him to me."

Rachel bent down and kissed his forehead. "Chief Rossiter still has work to do, so I'll come and get you in a little while."

He nodded, but he really wasn't listening.

"I'll bring him back, Rachel." The way he said her name in that deep voice reached to every atom of her body. "Mind if I call you that?"

She lifted her head. "Of course not. Thank you for being so wonderful to Nicky."

"Your nephew calls me Vance. Why don't you?"

The odd tension between them left her a little breathless. "I didn't know I had permission." Because he wore his wedding ring, she hadn't dared think of him as Vance.

"Our rocky beginning was my fault."

"No, I take full responsibility!" She rushed to settle the record.

"So let's start over, shall we?" With that, he gave his full attention to Nicky and hustled him out of the lodge.

Rachel watched them walk away. Nicky was so happy, he was half skipping and jumping. She found herself wishing she'd been included. However, when she realized it wasn't just because she was already missing Nicky, she groaned and hurried back to the room. It was a good thing they were leaving Yosemite.

In fact, thinking about tomorrow reminded her she needed to make a hotel reservation for them in Merced.

Walking over to the house phone, she called the front desk and asked them to take care of the arrangements. Once that was accomplished, she phoned her parents.

"Mom? Put Dad on the other extension. I want to tell you our plans for tomorrow."

"All right. Just a minute."

This was going to be hard for them to hear, but without Nicky in the room she could talk freely.

"Hi, honey," her dad said. "Go ahead."

"Tomorrow morning at seven, Nicky and I will be going up on top of El Capitan."

"Have you seen it yet?" Her mother's voice sounded pained.

"We passed it as we drove in."

"What's it like?"

"Tell you what. I'll read what's in the brochure." She picked it out of a pile left by the hotel. "'El Capitan is a three-thousand-foot monolith of coarse-grained granite. The Native Americans call it Totokanoola....' And the early Spaniards loosely translated that to mean 'Chief,'" she explained to her parents. How appropriate! Wait till she told Nicky.

"'Once considered impossible to climb, it is now the standard for Big Wall climbing the world over and has two main faces, the most famous being The Nose. You can get to the top by hiking out of Yosemite Valley on the trail next to Yosemite Falls.'"

Her mother sounded aghast. "You're not really thinking of taking Nicky up there—"

"Not hiking, Mom. The chief ranger, Vance Rossiter, has arranged for us to go in a helicopter with him and the pilot who was involved in the recovery mission."

"Was he the one in charge last year?" The sharpness

in her tone reminded Rachel of herself before she flew out to Yosemite with Nicky.

"Yes." She took a fortifying breath. "Since meeting him, my whole view of what happened to Ben and Michelle has changed. I have testimony that the rangers did everything in their power to warn him and Michelle off El Capitan before the storm hit, but you know how stubborn Ben can be when he's having fun." She bit her lip. "Nicky's just like him."

"I'm glad to hear you're not blaming them anymore, honey." This from her dad.

Tears spilled down her cheeks. "I've been wrong about a lot of things. What a fool I was not to have taken Dr. Karsh's advice a lot sooner. We've only been here a few days and already Vance has turned Nicky's world around. H-he's a very sensitive man who's been suffering over the accident, too," she stammered. "I have total confidence in his instincts to help Nicky understand what happened up there without frightening him."

Her mother moaned. "I don't know."

"I *do*, Mom. You're going to have to trust me on this. Nicky wants answers. This is an unprecedented opportunity to be with the two people who brought Ben and Michelle down. If Vance can't satisfy Nicky and calm his fears, then no one can."

"I'm all for it," her dad interjected. After clearing his throat he said, "Sounds like the headman has gone out of his way for you with his time and resources."

"He's been amazing. The other day he and Nicky flew in a helicopter to the other end of the park to go owl watching."

"You're kidding!" her mother cried.

"I didn't tell you before because I didn't want you worrying."

"Where's Nicky right now?"

"With Vance. We all went swimming this afternoon. Now he's over at headquarters having a root beer in his office."

Her father chuckled. "Sounds like he's having fun."

The word *fun* didn't cover it. She bowed her head. "He's having the time of his life."

"What about you, honey?"

Me? That's a good question. I've met a man who's bigger than life.

"This has been the therapy I've needed, too," she admitted. "One thing has become clear to me. I've done the right thing by giving up my job. Time is too short to keep making mistakes. Nicky needs me. I want to be his mother, and plan to find work close by the house so he won't ever feel abandoned again."

She could hear her parents weeping for joy. After Rachel composed herself she said, "I'll call you tomorrow from the Merced Inn."

"We'll be waiting, honey," her dad said.

Her mother sniffed. "What about Steven?"

Since she'd begun planning this trip, her ex-fiancé had been the furthest thing from her mind. "Dr. Karsh says I need to face him and work through my feelings. Maybe I will." After a pause she admitted, "Karsh was right about Nicky. No doubt he's right about this, too."

"We're behind you whatever you decide, honey."

"I know. I love you. Talk to you later."

The minute Rachel got off the phone, she sorted through the brochures to look for a good place to eat dinner. They'd spent enough time at the lodge. One pamphlet on Curry Village caught her eye. There were informal pizza and Mexican food eateries there, perfect for Nicky while they enjoyed different views of the Yosemite Valley. Then it would be early to bed.

Nicky was right about the national park being huge. They'd seen only a minute portion of it, but it was the part where her brother and sister-in-law had met with tragedy. After tomorrow, she and Nicky would leave the past behind them and—please, God—his nightmares would come to an end.

Feeling restless, she phoned hotel information for the headquarters number, then asked for the chief ranger's extension. They put her through.

"Chief Rossiter's office. Beth Henderson speaking."

"Hello. This is Rachel Darrow. I wonder if you can tell me if my nephew is still there?"

"He sure is. Do you want to talk to him?"

"No. Will you let him know I'm driving over there now to pick him up for dinner? Ask him to meet me out in front."

"Will do. He's so cute I'd like to take him home with me, but I think the chief would beat me to it."

Rachel smiled. If the truth be told, Nicky would go home with him willingly. "I hope that means he's been on his best behavior."

"Does he have any other kind?"

Unfortunately, Ranger Jarvis could give Vance's receptionist an earful. "You're very nice. Thank you. I'll be there in a minute."

After running a brush through her hair, she replenished her coral frost lipstick and left the hotel. As she got in the rental car, she could tell her heart was pounding. Not until she drove up in front of headquarters and saw the chief ranger in animated conversation with Nicky and one of the cute female rangers did she admit to the reason why.

"Rachel!" Nicky ran over to the driver's side of the car. She put the window down. "Guess what?"

"What?"

"Ranger Davis is in charge of the Junior Park Rangers. They're going to have a big party with a movie and food in the auditorium right now. Can I go?"

"Hi," the ranger said, darting Rachel a friendly smile. "They're all teenagers and will get a kick out of him. I'll bring him back to the chief's office when it's over."

"Well, thank you for the invitation. That sounds fun, Nicky. Be sure and mind her."

"I will. See ya later."

He ran after her and they disappeared inside the building. In a way Rachel felt relief that Nicky wanted to be with someone else other than Vance. She was sure he was relieved, too.

"May I have a lift to my house?"

Vance's question stunned her. A quiver of excitement shot through her body. "Yes, of course. Please get in. You'll have to point the way."

He directed her along the road past a copse of pines until they came to a cluster of houses. She drove down a couple of streets until he told her to pull into the driveway of his fifties-looking, ranch-style house.

She glanced over, waiting for him to get out, but he did the unexpected. "I'd like to talk to you in private and this may be our only opportunity. Come inside and I'll fix some enchiladas for us."

The invitation for Nicky to attend the junior rangers

party suddenly made sense. It provided the perfect baby-sitting service, but her nephew wouldn't have realized it.

While Rachel sat there, bemused by Vance's actions, he climbed from the car with enviable male grace and came around the other side to help her out. Their arms brushed, sending more currents of electricity through her nervous system.

Once he'd ushered her inside the front door, she took in the L-shaped living and dining room. The house had been decorated in a green-and-yellow-plaid motif with dark brown leather furniture. A man's home if there ever was one.

"The bathroom is down the hall if you want to freshen up later."

"Thank you."

She followed him through to the kitchen. It was large enough to accommodate a Swedish-designed pecan wood breakfast table and chairs. He kept his house more spotless than most women.

His gaze swept over her. "What can I get you to drink?"

"Nothing right now, thank you."

"Then have a seat." He washed his hands before pulling ingredients from the fridge.

"Let me help." She washed her hands, too.

A faint smile hovered on his lips. "I'll brown the meat if you'll make the salad."

For the next few minutes they both got busy. After their fiery start several days ago, it was hard to believe she was in the chief ranger's house, helping to prepare a meal with him in absolute harmony.

Their eyes met as he handed her an avocado. "Who would have thought we'd end up like this after you flew out of my office with justifiable rage the other morning?"

He could read minds, too. What else had he picked up on? "It was *not* my finest hour."

"Nor mine," he confessed in a husky tone. He fried the tortillas and filled them with ground beef and cheese. After he put them in the oven, he set the table. "I'm glad we're past that stage, because I have a proposition for you."

Rachel laughed gently. "Now what am I to deduce from that?" She discovered her legs had gone weak from proximity to him, and sought out the nearest chair. It was impossible not to watch the play of muscle across his back and shoulders as he moved about. His tall, powerful body dominated the room.

He lounged against the edge of the counter for a minute, turning on her the full force of his blue eyes. Because they were fringed by black lashes, the color stood out, almost making her own eyes water when she looked into them. "That all depends on what you'd like to deduce from it," he teased, revealing a sense of humor she wouldn't have attributed to him when they'd first met.

Again she was struck by the change in tension between them. This time there was no rancor, only an energy that was beginning to build.

Leaving her hanging, he served their meal, then sat down opposite her. They tucked into their food. She was hungry. "This tastes delicious."

"Thank you. Let's hope you approve enough to consider my job offer."

She blinked. A job?

"Compared to what you were making at the cruise line it's probably a pittance, but a truck and a vacant, furnished house for you and Nicky go with it."

Rachel stopped chewing. He just kept surprising her.

For some odd reason it disturbed her to realize he was thinking on a practical level rather than…

What a fool she was to forget for a second he was still married to his wife's memory. "I'm sorry Nicky ever brought up the subject."

He'd just devoured his fourth enchilada. "I'm glad he did. Ask any ranger and they'll tell you I've been looking for a liaison person to do a multitude of tasks. Beth had the job until I made her my private secretary. It has to be the right person, but she spoiled me for anyone else."

I can tell you right now I'm not the person you want.

"This isn't a desk job. I need someone not employed by the government or the Federal Park Service to be my eyes and ears around here. When you came to Yosemite, you had every right to want to bring me up on charges. I've been thinking about it ever since."

Her temper flared. "Vance—I've already apologized for that."

"I know, but what you brought up that day was and is important. A woman has special instincts and might foresee problems before they happen, especially where children are concerned. I'd welcome any safety recommendations from you. This summer Nicky could do it with you."

She put down her napkin. "Look—it's not that I'm not appreciative of what you're offering, but your strong sense of guilt over what happened to my brother and his wife has prompted you to come up with this idea."

"This has nothing to do with guilt," he declared.

Rachel averted her eyes, not knowing quite what to believe. "Well, thank you for considering me, but as I told you before, Nicky and I have a life back in Miami with my parents."

"And your ex-fiancé?"

Her eyes flicked to his in exasperation. "Nicky has done too much talking out of school."

Vance sat there looking insolently at ease, while she was trembling. "Only because he loves you and knows you were hurt. He's afraid you might go back to Steven. Is that why you're not willing to consider working here?"

She might have known Nicky would tell all to his favorite person in the world. "I don't honestly know what I'm going to do yet."

"Fair enough, but at least consider what I'm offering. If it's a possibility that could work out for you, in the future it could become a permanent position."

With those words her pain quadrupled. "That's very kind of you and I promise I'll think about it," she lied. After glancing at her watch, she said, "Let me help you with the dishes, then I've got to get back to headquarters to pick up Nicky."

With that she started clearing the table, but Vance stopped her from stacking the dishes in the dishwasher. "These will keep."

He was too close to her. "In that case, I'd better go."

"Rachel?"

She made the mistake of looking at him. The solemn expression in his eyes knocked her off balance. "Yes?"

"If I've angered you again, it wasn't intentional."

"Y-you didn't anger me," she stammered.

He folded his arms. "But I touched a nerve. Was it because I mentioned Steven?"

Time for a deep breath. "Not so much that. It's the idea that Nicky knows way too much."

"That's only natural. He loves you. You're his lifeline. Anything that affects you affects him in triplicate."

She smiled briefly. "If I didn't know it before we left Florida, I know it now. However, there's something else."

"Go ahead. Let's clear the air completely."

"Please don't take this wrong, but you do too much for him."

"And you resent it? Is that what you're saying?"

Rachel bit her lip. "No, not at all, but his memory of his father and his relationship with you are all blended together right now. He's confused."

"Believe me, I'm aware of that," Vance said in a sober tone. "Once you're back in Florida, he'll get it all straightened out in his mind. For the time being, it won't hurt if he's a little mixed up. I'd rather he clung to me emotionally while I take him up on El Capitan in the morning."

She should have realized Vance had a reason for everything he did. If she was having problems, it appeared they had more to do with her overwhelming attraction to him and nothing else.

Her moist eyes searched his for a timeless moment. "I'll never be able to thank you enough for what you've done for him. You're a remarkable man." On impulse she kissed his hard jaw, then reached for her purse and hurried out of the kitchen.

WITH HIS FINGERS, Vance felt the spot she'd just kissed. Though Rachel had meant the gesture to be a demonstration of gratitude, the touch of her lips sent sparks of desire through his sensitized body. Groaning inwardly, he raced after her, but she beat him to her car. They drove back to the visitors' center in silence.

"Wait here, Rachel. I'll get him."

He walked inside headquarters. The teens were just coming out of the auditorium. Nicky saw him and ran over, his cute face wreathed in a smile. "I wish I was a junior ranger. They have uniforms just like you."

"You like those, huh?" Vance chuckled. "Did you have fun?"

"Yup. The bears in that movie were really funny."

Vance reached for his hand and walked him outside, while Nicky chattered a mile a minute. Vance put him in the back in his car seat.

"What are you going to do now?" Nicky asked.

"He has work, honey," Rachel explained before Vance could. "We have other plans."

"Where are we going?"

"For a walk around Curry Village," she said with determination.

Vance would love to join them, but it would be like moving around in a goldfish bowl. The whole park would be watching. "They have great ice cream over there."

Nicky only eyed Vance mournfully. "Can't you come with us?"

He could feel Rachel begging him to back her up in this. "I'm afraid I have more park business to do," he lied. Of course there were always things needing to be done, but he didn't have anything pressing at the moment. "See you later, radiator." He leaned in the back window to high-five him, but Nicky had no interest in perpetuating their little word game.

Vance understood how he felt, because he was suffering from the same affliction. He waved to Rachel before heading back inside headquarters. It was going to be a long night.

No sooner did he enter his office than Beth told him Ranger Nelson was on line one. He reached for the phone. "What's up, Bob?"

"A fire has broken out in the Laurel Lakes basin."

"How widespread?"

"Maybe ten acres. We don't know yet if the culprit was lightning or campers. I've given the order to clear people out now."

"Close it all off, including the trail leading up to it from Miguel Meadow, and keep in touch with me."

"Yes, sir."

Natural wildfires were good for the park, helping the forest regenerate. However, if they grew out of control, then the rangers had to send in air tankers. In any given year they lost sixteen to twenty thousand acres of forest due to lightning strikes or prescribed, scheduled burns. For the moment Vance wasn't too concerned. Two other small fires were burning east of the Glacier Point area, but they were headed for containment and wouldn't interfere with tomorrow's flight to El Capitan. So far there was no undue cause for worry. At least not in that department.

He turned to his computer, situated at the right of his desk, to check the latest e-mails from various ranger stations. The notice about a bear incident in the Lower Pines Campground drew his attention and would have to be investigated.

As he scrolled down, his gaze fell on Timberwolf lying next to the keyboard. While Vance had been on the phone earlier, he'd let Nicky play on the Disney Web site. Rachel had taught him what to do. The boy was very computer savvy for one so young.

Vance picked up the little action figure, fingering it absently as he mentally replayed the day's events. Certain images filled his head and wouldn't leave. Rachel was a great sport. When he'd dunked her in the pool, she'd done her best to dunk him back. He could still feel the contact of their arms and legs. Her laughter had been as spontaneous as her smile. It lit up her whole countenance so he couldn't take his eyes off her.

While she'd done a backstroke race with Nicky, the lovely contours of her face and body had trapped the air in his lungs. Unaffected and ultrafeminine, Rachel possessed too many assets that spoke to Vance, making her unforgettable. He could still feel her kiss along his jaw.

Inhaling sharply, he jumped up from the desk, needing to redirect his energy by doing something worthwhile. Before he went home, he might as well get a firsthand report from Ranger Hollis about the bear incident. After pocketing Nicky's toy, he said goodnight to Beth and left headquarters.

When he entered the information center, it didn't surprise him to see Chase still on duty. Vance walked over to his desk. "What are you doing here?"

"What do you think?" Work was the panacea for both of them, but you couldn't do it twenty-four hours nonstop. Not even Chase, who had the strongest work ethic Vance had ever witnessed.

"I hear you." Vance was doing the same thing, by putting off being alone with his own torturous thoughts. Since Chase's divorce, the man had his own.

"Hey, Chief!" Hollis called to him. "It's all over the park how you took care of those inebriated college guys at the pool today." The two younger rangers were grinning at him. "How about giving us a quick course in the Rossiter technique?"

The park grapevine traveled faster than lightning. "You guys are full of it. How about you giving me the facts about the bear incident this morning."

"It wasn't the park's greatest moment. The bear and her two cubs climbed into a tall Jeffrey pine. They were up there quite a while. Then the cubs started to back down. When the sow realized she'd gotten separated from them, she began to get aggressive. We feared she would attack the campers gathered around, so we had to tranquilize her."

"I'm glad you didn't have to do worse." If her cubs were threatened, a mother bear turned killer. It was instinct. Rachel had that same instinct where Nicky was concerned.

"Me, too. We called Fish and Game. They came and transported the family for release."

"I'll make certain the official report reaches the superintendent, with a carbon copy to the park publicist. The newspapers will still print an animal cruelty headline and leave out the fact that lives were threatened, but I can always live in hope for the truth to be revealed." He turned to Chase. "Want to get out of here?"

"I thought you'd never ask." He shoved himself away from the desk and stood up. They left the other rangers in charge and walked outside. "Feel like tacos?" Chase was referring to Curry Village, across the road, of course.

Bad idea. Little did Chase know the place was calling to Vance like a siren. "Why not come to my house? I have leftover enchiladas I can warm up for you."

Chase squinted at him. "You're sure you want to do that tonight?"

"It beats Nancy cornering us at the restaurant for another lecture on why bachelors don't live as long as married men."

They headed toward their housing area near the village complex. "Maybe that's because the women we want aren't available."

"Nope." Rachel was going back to Florida to be with her ex-fiancé. His proposition had been turned down flat.

"You sounded like Nicky just then," Chase observed. "I take it you two had fun at the pool."

"Yup. He's a great little swimmer." Vance started walking faster. They needed to switch topics. Soon the park would see the backs of Nicky and Rachel Darrow. He didn't want to think about it yet.

"I don't envy you taking him up on El Cap tomorrow. Let's hope the experience doesn't add to his nightmares."

"I guess the family will find out after he gets back to Florida," Vance muttered. Unfortunately, Rachel's psychiatrist wasn't infallible.

Rachel…

How long would that name resonate with him? He hoped and prayed not long, or the summer he'd been looking forward to would turn into early winter.

THE SUN'S RAYS HADN'T YET penetrated the depths of Yosemite Valley, but Rachel felt relief that a beautiful, calm summer morning had dawned. Mixed in with the dread of reliving her brother's tragedy was this undeniable excitement at the thought of being with Vance one more time.

Nicky couldn't wait to see him, and was too worked up to eat breakfast. Just in case he got hungry later on, she stashed some snacks and a juice box in her purse. They both put on a lightweight jacket over their Levi's and pullovers, then left for the lobby. Nicky let out a whoop when he saw Vance through the glass.

In full uniform, the chief ranger looked every inch the part as he lounged against the truck with his arms folded, waiting for them. The second Nicky shot out the doors, Vance was there to pick him up and help him inside the cab. Then he reached for Rachel. The sun hadn't spilled its rays on them yet. In shadow, the eyes trained on her appeared a darker blue than usual.

"Good morning." For some reason his voice sounded an octave lower than she remembered. This was one mission neither of them had been looking forward to, but she sensed there was something else bothering him.

"Good morning." Her greeting came out more like a whisper before he assisted her in and shut the door.

The drive to the helipad only took a few minutes. Thankfully, Nicky's chatter covered over the awkwardness. Vance had an almost forbidding aura about him this morning. Naturally, he wanted this experiment to work, but in its own way this had to be hauntingly painful for him, too.

Several rangers belonging to the search and rescue team were there to greet them. Nicky stood between her and Vance, gripping the hands of both. The pilot hunkered down in front of him. "Hi, Nicky. My name's Perry. I'm the man who helped the chief find your parents. I'll be flying us up to the top of El Capitan. Are you ready?"

"Yup." That little word had so many meanings. It could convey he was so happy he couldn't talk, or he was bored, or he was terrified. If he felt like she did, the third definition covered it all.

"Then let's be off. The chief will strap you in." Perry stood up and looked at Rachel. "Ms. Darrow? If you'll climb in back first and buckle up."

She did his bidding, followed by Nicky, who kept his eyes on Vance's face and listened to every word while he was being buckled in.

"I have to sit in front, but once we get up there I'll keep hold of you every second. Is that okay with you?" the chief said.

Nicky nodded.

"You're going to see the whole Yosemite Valley. It's a sight not many six-year-olds get to see from that vantage point."

"Did you go up there when you were six?"

"Nope. Not until I was ten."

The wheels were turning. "Was it scary?" he asked in all earnestness.

Rachel saw the difficulty Vance had in swallowing. "Yes, but it was so awesome I forgot to be frightened. Your parents thought it was so awesome, they didn't want to come down."

Nicky's hazel eyes suddenly brightened. Vance had found the right words. "Yeah."

"Yeah." His hero smiled.

Like the tiny leaves of a seed that suddenly sprouted from the ground, admiration, even love for the chief ranger sprang into Rachel's being. There was an innate honesty in him tempered with a goodness and uncanny insight that was on a higher level than the people around him. She saw it in the respect everyone who worked in the park had for him. In Nicky's case he inculcated absolute trust.

"Are you ready, sport?"

"Let's go!"

"You heard the man, Perry."

Once Vance strapped himself in the copilot's seat and put on headgear, the rotors started to turn. Rachel hadn't flown in a helicopter before. She'd confided as much to Nicky last night. He must have remembered their conversation, because he looked over at her. "Don't be scared, Rachel. Vance won't let anything happen to us."

"I know." *I know.*

Plucked from the ground like an eagle's prey, the helicopter carried them off, leaving her stomach behind. Her hands gripped the armrests. She didn't think she took another breath until they were heading straight across the open valley for El Capitan. The sun gilded part of its face, making the moment surreal.

"Whoa. It's huge!" Nicky cried. He'd used that word often in connection with the park.

Vance turned on the microphone. "We're almost there. If you look closely, Nicky, you'll see people climbing with ropes." Rachel strained to pick them out. She couldn't imagine attempting to scale anything that sheer.

"They look like ants! Did my mommy and daddy do that?"

"No," he answered. "See that trail on your right? Like a ribbon coming along that high ridge?"

"Yes?"

"That's the path they took to hike over from Tamarack Flats so they'd be right on top. We're going to land where they were camped."

Like a tuft of cotton coming to rest, the pilot set them down on the enormous, flat white rock. Being there wasn't as frightening as she'd anticipated. That was because they weren't near the edge.

Vance carried Nicky in his arms. So far her nephew seemed fine. "What do you think?" the chief asked him.

"Are we at the top of the world?"

Both men smiled.

"It feels like it," Perry commented. "What else do you want to ask us?"

Nicky cupped Vance's face. "Can I get down and walk around?"

"As long as you hold my hand."

"I will." Once he was lowered to the ground he looked at Rachel. "Will you hold my hand, too?"

Her heart melted as she grasped it. Together the three of them moved wherever Vance led them. He was careful to stay away from the edge. In the distance they could hear the occasional shout of a climber calling to a companion. The sun was out in full force now. Rachel looked around in wonder, feeling as if they were standing at the edge of creation.

"How come it's still cold?" Nicky asked.

Vance stopped walking. "Because we're up seventy-five hundred feet. It's always twenty degrees cooler up here than at the valley floor. That's why the storms on top are so much worse when they move in."

Nicky grew pensive. "I bet when it snowed my mommy and daddy got really, really cold."

"They did, but remember they had each other to help them stay warm until they went to sleep."

Vance...

"That's 'cause they loved each other, huh."

A wealth of emotion forced Rachel to hug him hard. "Just the way they loved you."

He hugged her back. They stayed that way for a long time. When he finally let her go, he turned to Vance. "Where did you take my mommy and daddy?"

"Perry flew all of us down to the village. Then a special car took them to the airport, where they were flown back to your grandparents in Miami."

His head whipped around. He stared at Rachel. "I didn't see them."

"Neither did I, darling. Nana and Papa had them buried in the cemetery."

"What's that?"

"You don't remember going there?"

"No."

"Then we'll visit their graves as soon as we get home."

Vance picked him back up. "Tell you what. Since you're leaving for Merced, I'll ask your aunt to take the route through Oakhurst. We'll stop so you can see the cemetery where my parents and grandparents are buried. I want to put some flowers on my grandma's grave. You can help me decide what kind."

Nicky's face brightened. "My nana loves yellow roses the best."

"Then that's what we'll buy."

"Is Katy buried there, too?"

"No. Her grave is in Fullerton, California, next to her grandpa's."

"Do you put flowers on her grave, too?"

Rachel's heart lurched.

"Whenever I get the chance to visit."

"Is it a long way?"

"Not as far as it is to Florida."

His blond head swung around to Rachel. "Can we put yellow roses on Mommy and Daddy's graves, too?"

Tears blinded her. "We'll put on a whole bunch of them!"

"Vance? When we go to your house can I ride in your truck with you?"

"I was hoping you'd ask, but it's up to your aunt."

"Can I, Rachel?"

It was going to make the final parting from Vance that much harder for Nicky, but knowing they were leaving today, she wouldn't have refused him for anything in the world. "Of course."

"Can we go back now? I'm hungry and I want to talk on the microphone in his truck."

"I can fix the hungry part right now." After opening her purse she handed each of them a Kit Kat bar. "Do you want your juice?" He nodded. "Here you go."

Never in her wildest dreams would she have imagined Nicky enjoying a snack with Vance on top of El Capitan. It took away the terrible sadness she'd carried for so long.

"Everyone smile," Perry said before snapping some pictures of the three of them. Vance had thought of everything. Her parents would want to see these. As for Rachel, she'd treasure them forever.

When the pilot had finished, Rachel walked over to him. "I'd like to get one of you with them. In our family, you're a real hero."

"Happy to oblige."

While she was at it, she took pictures of the helicopter and their surroundings. When she returned the camera to him, she gave him a hug. "Words can't express what you did for my brother and his wife, let alone what you've done for Nicky. Please know I'll always be in your debt."

"Just doing my job." He was modest, like Vance. "This has helped *me*," he said sincerely.

Rachel believed him. "I think we're ready to go now," she murmured with a tremulous smile. Yet even as she said it, she felt the pain of parting. That was one emotion she hadn't expected to take away when they left Yosemite for good.

Chapter Six

Two hours later Rachel, Nicky and Vance had eaten a big breakfast and were ready to leave for Oakhurst. When she went out to the front desk to settle her bill, she discovered it had already been taken care of.

She turned to Vance, who'd helped Nicky take their bags to the car. Right now they were in the foyer looking at the owl. "I happen to know your job doesn't give you an expense account."

His eyes glimmered mysteriously. "Sometimes there are exceptions." Meaning he'd paid for it out of his own pocket.

Lowering her voice, she said, "I can't let you do this."

"It's done. Don't rob me of the pleasure of easing your financial burden in some small way. After all you've suffered, I'd do it again. For Nicky…"

Rachel averted her eyes. "I know you would, because you're an extraordinary person."

"The feeling's mutual."

On trembling legs she walked over to Nicky. "Let's go."

Vance transferred Nicky's car seat to the truck. A minute later they were on their way. Her nephew waved to her through the window of the power wagon. She followed in the rental car, careful not to let any other vehicles get between them.

Throughout the drive to Oakhurst, Nicky called her every so often on Vance's cell phone in order to tell her some new tidbit he'd learned about the park from his mentor.

"Did you know some of the traffic rangers ride motorcycles?"

"I saw one pass us going the other way," she replied.

"Yeah. Vance said a car was speeding and the driver would get a ticket."

"Uh-oh."

"I wish I could see him get mad."

She could hear Vance chuckling in the background. The sound thrilled her. "Darling? Guess what I found out?"

"What?" Nicky asked excitedly.

"El Capitan is Spanish for an Indian word, and I know what it means in English."

"Is it captain?"

"Something even greater."

"Superintendon?"

Rachel broke into laughter. "No. Something much more important."

"What is it?" He'd run out of guesses.

"Chief!"

There was a pregnant pause. "You mean like Vance?" She could almost hear him add, "The greatest guy on earth?"

"Exactly!"

"Whoa!" Rich male laughter rang through the phone.

"Hey, Vance—"

She smiled because Nicky had forgotten he was

talking to her. Totally amused by his chatter, she left her phone on speaker mode until he remembered he was still connected.

"Vance says we're almost there. See you in a minute." He hung up.

They passed the sign for Oakhurst. Before long the truck pulled up in front of an attractive ranch-style house with a stone and siding exterior. As she came to a stop and parked, Vance walked back to her.

He leaned down, giving her the full force of eyes a more brilliant blue than the sky. "I phoned the people renting my grandparents' house. They'll keep an eye on your car until we get back from the cemetery."

With his help she got out and locked it. He ushered her around to the passenger side of the truck and opened the door. Their arms and hips brushed as she squeezed inside, making her acutely aware of him. When Nicky gave her a quick hug she held on to him to get herself under some kind of control.

"This is where Vance used to live!"

"I know. It's a lovely home. Kind of reminds me of Nana and Papa's house."

"Yeah," Nicky agreed. "Where are we going to get roses?"

Vance started up the truck. "There's a florist a couple of blocks over."

"Can I help pick them out?"

Rachel's gaze collided with Vance's before he said, "I was counting on it."

Since this morning she was forced to acknowledge a new dynamic at play involving Nicky. She had a presentiment the parting with Vance was going to be traumatic, and she wasn't looking forward to it.

Once they arrived at the florist, she remained in the truck while the two of them went inside. No matter Nicky's expectations, she wouldn't allow them to linger at the cemetery. They needed to be gone from Yosemite and put this chapter of their lives behind them before she forgot that Vance was still wearing his wedding ring. As for the chief, he needed to get back on the job. It was a miracle he'd given them this much time.

Out of the corner of her eye she saw Nicky come out the front door, carrying a container with a dozen yellow roses. The whole bouquet was bigger than he was. Vance put it in the truck bed, then they got inside.

Rachel kissed her nephews cheek. "Those are the prettiest flowers I've ever seen."

"Vance says his grandma will love them."

"No doubt about it."

A mile and a half away, they entered the cemetery, which was kept in immaculate condition.

"I've seen cemeteries before!" Nicky announced.

"I'm sure you have, darling." Maybe he was remembering. Many of the graves had flags and flowers. It hadn't been that long since Memorial Day.

"Here we are." Vance stopped along the side of the lane, turned off the motor and helped Nicky jump down. The little boy ran over to one of the markers. "What are these?"

"Headstones."

"Headstones?"

Rachel went to join him. "Yes. They show the names and the dates of people who died. Snow and rain won't damage them."

Vance carried the roses to a light gray tombstone

that had two names inscribed. Nicky hurried after him. "Is this where your grandma and grandpa are buried?"

"That's right." He placed the flowers in the center.

Nicky sounded out their names. "Dor-o-thy and Wil-liam Ross-iter."

"Good for you," Vance praised. "What are your grandparents' names?"

He hesitated. "Nana and Papa Darrow."

Rachel put her hands on his shoulders. "Minnie and Ted."

"Oh, yeah, but my mommy and daddy's names are Benjamin and Michelle." He looked up at her. "Do they have a headstone?"

"Yes. As soon as we get home, we'll pick some yellow roses from the garden and go right over so you can see it."

She knew his next question before it left his lips. "Can Vance come with us?"

"I'm afraid not." Rachel answered as calmly as possible. They'd talked this over a dozen times already. "He lives here and he's in charge of the whole park. In fact, he has to drive back right now. Let's go, darling." She grasped his hand and headed for the truck.

To her relief he didn't put up an argument. They all got in the cab and headed back to Vance's grandparents' house without incident. It wasn't until they were parked in front of her car that she understood why there'd been no histrionics yet.

"Why can't we stay with Vance? He has a house in the park and lives all alone," Nicky argued.

She pretended not to hear him, and opened the door. "Come on." When he wouldn't budge, she removed his resisting body from the car seat and carried him to her rental vehicle. Unfortunately, she needed her keys, which were in her purse.

Vance caught up to them with the car seat and gathered Nicky in his arms so she could unlock the door.

"I don't want to go." By now tears were pouring down the boy's cheeks. He buried his face in Vance's neck, releasing great heaving sobs. This was one time when the ranger couldn't make it better, not with all his potent hero magic. The sooner she drove away, the better.

But he had to put Nicky down while he installed the car seat in the back. If anyone saw the three of them right now, they'd call 9-1-1, thinking something terrible was going on. Nicky was out of control. When Vance strapped him in, he screamed harder and kicked his legs. "I don't want to go! I want to stay with you!"

"I wish you could, sport." Rachel could swear she heard tears in Vance's voice. This was a nightmare of new proportions. "I'll call you when I get back in my truck, and we'll talk while we both drive." He shut the door.

Nicky wasn't listening. He only sobbed harder. His heart was breaking and neither of them could do anything about it. This was almost worse than the trauma of a year ago.

Rachel lifted pained eyes to Vance. "Thank you for everything," she said, before starting the car. He stood there, looking so helpless and grim she could hardly bear it.

"Nooo!" Nicky shouted when she drove away. "Vance!" he screamed. "Stop!"

Rachel was frantic and honestly didn't know what to do. Five seconds later her phone rang. She clicked on. "Vance?" she said in a trembling voice.

"I can't let things end this way, Rachel. I'm following you to Merced. Put Nicky on."

Deep inside she knew that spending any more time with him was only delaying the inevitable, and would make the situation even more intolerable. But she couldn't think beyond calming Nicky down.

She signaled before pulling off to the side of the road. Undoing her seat belt, she turned to him. "Vance has decided to drive as far as Merced with us before he has to go back. Do you want to talk to him?"

Nicky hiccuped. "Yes." His face was so blotchy he looked like he had giant hives.

Rachel leaned over the seat and handed the phone to him. Little by little his one-syllable answers turned into two words, then three. Before she knew it he was laughing. The calm after the storm enabled her to start driving again. Vance swung in behind her. He and Nicky kept up their conversation all the way into Merced, where they hit the late Saturday afternoon traffic.

"Vance says to follow him to the Merced Inn. He knows where *everything* is."

"You're right." Nicky must have told him where they were staying. "You have to hang up now."

"Okay. See you later, escalator."

Things were temporarily back to normal.

"Rachel? Can Vance take me to get my hair cut?"

She blinked. Where had that come from? She couldn't keep up with him. "A haircut?"

"Yup. Some of the kids in the pool said I have curls like a girl."

He did for a fact. "Did it hurt your feelings?"

"Yup. I told Vance. He said he had long black curls when he was my age 'cause his mommy liked them, but the kids teased him, so his daddy took him to the barber. I want to look just like Vance!"

What red-blooded American boy wouldn't? A military cut on Nicky ought to be something to see. "We don't have time to do that, honey."

"Please? I promise I'll be good and won't cry anymore."

That was a big promise, but maybe it would work.

"You really mean it?"

"Yes," he said, albeit tentatively.

His nana was going to cry when she saw the change in him. In fact her parents would be astonished by his new, confident demeanor. Rachel had discovered that the right man could work wonders for a vulnerable child missing his father.

Hopefully, Nicky would remember what he'd just told her, so they could go back to Florida without hysterics. But as she'd found out several days ago, Vance was an impossible act to follow.

THE BARBER REMOVED the drape fastened around Nicky's neck. "All finished, young man."

He jumped down. "How do I look?"

Vance barely recognized him. The little boy was gone. In his place was the promise of the man within. Vance patted his shoulder. "Tough! I like it. Are you ready to walk me to my truck?"

"Y-yes," he answered mournfully.

That was the deal between him and Nicky. If the boy promised not to cry or get upset when Vance left for the park, he would take him to get his hair cut and Nicky could call him on the phone from Miami whenever he wanted. Vance had written his cell phone number on a piece of paper for Nicky to keep in his pocket.

Vance paid the barber before they walked outside

to Rachel's car, where she was waiting. He'd left the truck at the hotel so they wouldn't have to move the car seat again.

After Nicky got in, she rubbed his head experimentally. "Do I know you?"

He giggled. "I'm me!"

"You sound like you," she teased, flashing Vance a laughing glance before starting the car. For a brief moment her smile lit him up inside. The thought of her getting back with her ex was anathema to him now.

A couple of minutes later they reached the Merced Inn and drove around to the parking area where her room was located. She pulled up next to his truck and turned off the motor.

Now that the moment of parting had come, the shoe seemed to be on the other foot. Vance was the one who felt like kicking and screaming. The Darrows had only been at Yosemite since Tuesday night. He hadn't met them until Wednesday morning. How in four days' time could he have come to care about them like this? So much that he felt as if his life were falling apart?

Not since he'd heard the news about Katy had he experienced feelings this emotionally wrenching. Was this what Chief Dick had seen in his vision? A big change that would affect him adversely for the rest of his life?

At the moment, Nicky appeared to be handling everything much better than Vance, or even Rachel, who'd been unusually quiet since their arrival in Merced.

Nicky scrambled out of the car. He waited for Vance to emerge from the front seat before diving into him with one of those bone-crushing hugs. Vance saw telltale moisture on the boy's eyelashes, but true to his promise, he held back any sobs.

Vance high-fived him. "See you in a while, crocodile."

Always quick to adapt, Nicky said, "See you in a while, reptile."

Vance noticed that it brought a smile to Rachel's lips. The desire to taste them was so strong, he turned abruptly away from her and got in the truck.

After switching on the motor, he glanced at both of them standing a few feet away. The sight would be indelibly impressed in his mind from here on out. "Have a safe flight, you two."

All the way to the other side of the continent. He didn't know how he was going to handle it.

Rachel flashed him the kind of smile that hid a myriad of emotions. He couldn't tell if she was having trouble watching him leave or not. "We'll be fine. I'm just worried you might drive too fast trying to get back to the park, and one of those motorcycle rangers will give you a ticket."

Nicky looked up at her in horror. "They wouldn't give one to *Vance*. He's the chief!"

Vance laughed in spite of his turmoil. "Give me a call tomorrow night and let me know you got home okay."

"Okay." His lower lip trembled. "Bye, Vance. Thanks for everything."

"You're welcome. Oh, I almost forgot." He reached into his pocket for Timberwolf. "You left this in my office." Nicky stared at it but didn't take it. "Isn't this your favorite toy?"

"Yes, but you can have it, if you want," he said quietly.

"I want," Vance said in a husky tone. He closed his hand around it.

"Goodbye, Vance." Rachel sounded equally moved. She mouthed her thanks one more time before he put the truck in gear and drove away.

If he hadn't had a string of phone calls to deal with, the return trip would have constituted the drive from hell. He talked to the pilot first.

"Thanks for what you did today, Perry."

"I didn't know if he'd be able to handle it or not, but as we found out, some kids are more resilient than grown-ups."

"You're right. I'm hoping his nightmares will end."

"Me, too. Just so you know, I e-mailed you the pictures we took on top of El Cap. Thought you'd like to send them to him."

"He'll love them." Vance would also send the pictures they'd taken at the Tuolomne Meadows. "Thanks, Perry."

"You're welcome. He's a cute little guy. Between you and me, he's got a knockout aunt. Whew."

Vance pressed on the accelerator. "Yup. Thanks again for giving up your morning."

"No problem. Talk to you later."

The second they finished speaking, he phoned Bob, who informed him that fifty acres in the Laurel Lakes area had now burned.

Vance said, "The number isn't alarming yet, but if the wind picks up we'll have to call in more firefighters. Keep me posted."

After dealing with a couple of scheduling problems, he came to the last message. It was from Chase. He phoned him back. "Sorry I couldn't return your call at the time. This has been quite a day." Without preamble he brought Chase up to date on everything. "Nicky finally calmed down enough to say goodbye without falling apart."

"I knew it wouldn't be pretty. Earlier I talked to Perry. He said Nicky was a trooper up there, but it was all because of you."

"The boy is missing his father. He poured out his emotions on me, but he'll be fine once he's back with his grandparents."

"My guess is things won't work out with Rachel and her ex. Nicky won't stand for it."

"That's what I'm hoping." The mere idea of anyone else trying to father Nicky sent Vance's blood pressure through the roof. As for Rachel's ex-fiancé marrying her… He stifled a groan.

"How far away are you?"

"I passed through the entrance a few minutes ago."

"Then come straight to my house. We'll catch the Angels-Mariners game from Seattle on the tube. I'll put steaks on."

"No food for me tonight. I've lost my appetite, but the game sounds good. See you soon." Anything to get his mind off Rachel.

WHEN RACHEL WALKED into her boss's office in Miami on Tuesday morning, she didn't expect to find her sandy-haired ex-fiancé sitting behind the desk. The second he saw her he jumped to his feet. After spending time with the chief ranger, she found Steven's six-foot height didn't seem very tall.

"Don't be angry. I asked Harry if I could have a few minutes with you first," he said. Nothing was sacred with Steven.

Rachel sat down in front of the desk. He looked thinner, overworked, but no less attractive with those conventionally handsome looks. "I'm not angry, but if you're here to try to talk me out of resigning, you're too late." So much had changed in a week's time, she felt like an entirely different person.

The guilty pain in his brown eyes seemed real enough. "Did your parents tell you I dropped by last week?"

"Yes."

Lines of anxiety marred his features. "I'm here to tell you I love you and want us to start over, but I don't know how to prove that what I did will never, ever happen again. I swear it, Rachel."

She took a deep breath. "I believe that you believe it. For your information, Nicky's psychiatrist has urged me to explore my feelings for you. He's convinced Ben and Michelle's deaths came too close on the heels of our breakup for me to work through all my emotions. When I left for California with Nicky, I fully intended to come home and call you."

"Sweetheart…" The hope in that one endearment was revealing. He started around the desk. Another second and he would reach her, but she moved faster and stood behind her chair.

Seeing him again didn't stir up her desire. On the contrary, she shrank from any contact. What she saw was a weak man who'd made love to his former girlfriend on the eve of his wedding to Rachel. She didn't care about the reason. All she knew was that Steven's commitment to her hadn't stood the test of their engagement, let alone a marriage meant to last a lifetime.

Maybe it wasn't fair to measure him against someone like Vance Rossiter, but she couldn't imagine the chief ranger doing something that unforgivable to the woman who held his heart. He still loved his deceased wife enough to wear his wedding ring. If that wasn't testimony of his regard for their marriage…

In every way Rachel found him to be an honorable man. She'd seen him under attack. When she'd unleashed her pain and anger on him, there'd been no retaliation. Instead he'd done what needed doing by seeking out Nicky to comfort him. That response had shown Vance to be a breed apart from any male she'd ever known.

Ask her nephew, who'd been inconsolable since the two of them had arrived home Sunday evening. There was only one man in his life, the supreme ruler of his universe. Steven would be invisible to Nicky now. No other man would satisfy, at least not in the foreseeable future. But the ramifications would have to be worried about another day.

Steven stood there motionless. "You won't even let me touch you?"

She shook her head. "I can't. When I gave you back the ring, I was in a tremendous amount of pain. Seeing you now proves to me my feelings have died. The truth is, I haven't missed you, Steven. It really is over. I know in my heart that no amount of therapy is going to change that."

"Wait a minute—I thought you said you were going to call me when you got back from your trip!" he challenged. "What happened in Yosemite to change your mind?"

"Nothing," she said, her gaze unwavering. "I just didn't expect to find you here in Harry's office. The truth is, I feel nothing where you're concerned. This has saved me trying to get in touch with you."

"You're lying, Rachel. I know you too well. You've met another man." His cheeks had turned a ruddy color.

Yes, she'd met another man, but he wasn't available. "I guess I shouldn't be surprised you'd leap to that conclusion, not after your history with Lynette." Her salvo connected, causing him to stay where he was. "Isn't it interesting you have yet to ask me about Nicky or how the trip affected him? The situation is always about you, because you inevitably twist things around so you're the victim."

His eyes narrowed. "That was below the belt, wasn't it?"

"I'm sorry if the truth hurts." Vance or no Vance, she'd moved on emotionally and couldn't go back.

He shook his head. "You're different. Who's the guy?"

She folded her arms. "I can see you'd like there to be one. Otherwise I've come to my senses on my own."

"Rachel…!"

Once upon a time he could have said her name in that intense way and she would have melted. "I wish you well, Steven, but if you don't mind, Nicky's waiting for me at home. Will you please send Harry back in so we can conclude business?"

"I won't accept this as final!" he blurted.

Obviously not. His pride was having a hard time.

She walked to the door. Looking over her shoulder, she said, "Tell Harry I'll call him."

Harry and Steven played golf together. Nothing was private between them. That explained why her boss had conveniently disappeared. In so doing, he'd removed any guilt she might have felt by not remaining to keep her appointment.

It was cathartic to leave the company, knowing the pain of the past was well and truly behind her. But like entering a revolving door, she'd been thrust through the other side into a growing new crisis with Nicky. The trip to Yosemite might have succeeded in reducing his nightmares, but he had a new fixation in the form of the park's chief ranger.

Within five minutes of running into the house to hug his grandparents Sunday evening, Nicky had begged

Rachel to get Vance on the phone. "He's waiting for me to call him. Here's his number." When he produced the slip of paper Vance had given him, she had no choice but to acknowledge it.

"I'll let you call him when you're in bed, not before." They were home now. No more indulging him. For the past week he'd been running her life. It had to stop.

Finally, at bedtime, she went into his room with the phone. Not wanting Vance to think the call was her idea, she pressed the digits, then handed Nicky the phone and left the bedroom. A few minutes later she and her mother peeked in, only to discover he was still on the line, giggling like the carefree child he'd been before his parents' deaths.

"I have to admit I'm grateful to that man for turning Nicky around," her mom whispered.

"So am I, but I'm worried Nicky's going to think he can talk to him all the time."

"Don't be too concerned. You just got home. We'll take him to the cemetery tomorrow and arrange for Blake to come over in the afternoon. In a day or two he'll settle down. Knowing you've quit your job has made a big difference in his behavior. That look of anxiety on his face has disappeared."

Yes, Rachel had noticed, but she gave all the credit to Vance, who'd made Nicky feel cherished and safe, exactly the way a father would have done, the way Ben had done.

After leaving the cruise line parking lot earlier today, she'd headed for the supermarket. Once she'd picked up some groceries and her dad's refill at the pharmacy, she'd driven home, hoping Nicky was enjoying being over at Blake's house. He needed the interaction with friends.

"Rachel, honey?" her father called to her when he heard her enter the kitchen from the garage. She put the bags down and went into the dining room, where he was sitting at the table in front of the laptop.

"Where's Mom?"

"She went to pick up Nicky."

"It's only lunchtime. I was hoping he'd play longer."

"He wanted to come home in case Vance phoned."

No surprise there. "I was afraid of that, but Vance is too busy to be bothered."

"Nevertheless, Mr. Rossiter phoned the house a while ago to get our e-mail address."

Her pulse ran away with her. "You talked to him?"

"I surely did. We had quite a conversation. Nicky told me he was a marine. He's an impressive man dealing with heavy responsibilities. I'd planned to phone him and thank him for all his help with Nicky. His call saved me the trouble.

"Take a look at these pictures he sent. There's one of Nicky up on top of El Capi—" He was so choked up he couldn't talk.

She stepped behind him and looked over his shoulder. In the photo on-screen Nicky looked like Ben at that age. It was precious. Her father scrolled down and landed on one of Vance gazing at Nicky while they walked around on top of the flat rock. There was an expression on his rugged face that could only be described as love. Nicky was staring up at him in worship.

Her dad made a sound in his throat. "Will you look at that."

Since last Wednesday Rachel had been a witness to that uncanny rapport between them. Was it just a week ago the chief ranger had entered the lodge dining room to talk to Nicky? What transpired during that conversation had righted his world and quieted his fears.

"Rachel?" She turned to see Nicky run into the dining room with her mom at his heels. "Did Vance call? He said he was going to."

"As a matter of fact he did," her father answered. "He wanted our e-mail address so he could send us some pictures. Look—there you are with him and Rachel."

Nicky nestled close to his papa to view everything. All kinds of excited noises came out of him.

Her mother teared up. "I'm glad these were taken before you turned into a junior marine."

Rachel gave her a hug. They both mourned the loss of his curls.

When they'd seen all the pictures, Nicky whipped his head around to look up at her. "I want to call him back."

"We can't right now." She could feel a tug-of-war coming on. Never again. "Did you have fun with Blake?"

"I guess." He pressed his grandpa's arm. "Will you call him? I have his number." He pulled it out of his pocket. The little monkey kept it on him at all times.

Ted eyed Rachel and his wife before he said, "I'll let you call him this time, to thank him for the pictures."

"Hooray! I love you." The boy kissed his cheek.

"I love you, too, but Rachel's right. Vance is in charge of everything that happens in the park and doesn't have a lot of free time to talk. We have to honor that."

Nicky sobered. "But last night he said I could 'cause I'm his favorite person."

"Well, that's a real compliment," her father commented.

"What does that word mean?"

Rachel squeezed his shoulders. "It means you're lucky that a wonderful man like him cares so much about you."

"He said he loves me."

"Who wouldn't?"

Stunned that Vance had used those exact words, she hugged him to cover her concern. Nicky took everything literally. In his mind if Vance loved him, then he had permission to be a part of his life. That meant instant access.

This wasn't good. No wonder he was so insistent on talking to Vance. *What to do?* Rachel needed some advice about now.

Dr. Karsh had told her to call him after they got back. She'd planned to, but hadn't expected to be forced to consult him this soon. Unfortunately, Vance's declaration of affection for her innocent nephew had upped the timetable.

She leaned down to whisper in her dad's ear. "While you phone Vance, I'll go to my room and give Dr. Karsh a call. Maybe I'll be lucky enough to reach him on his lunch hour."

He patted her arm, letting her know it was a good idea. The deaths of Ben and Michelle had been final, but the chief ranger was alive and as far away as a phone call.

Chapter Seven

Once the ambulance left the scene, Vance walked around the two buses that had collided on the road inside the Tioga Pass entrance. Though the Sierra Trails tour bus had been damaged, no one on board had been injured. Another bus was on the way to pick up the tourists, so they could continue their vacation through the park.

Due to admitted driver error, a busful of high school students leaving the park had taken a bigger hit. Three of the teens had suffered minor injuries and been taken to the hospital to be checked out. The rest of the group had been shuttled back to Bishop, California, where their trip had originated.

All in all, Vance could be thankful there'd been no fatalities or anything close to it this morning. He was talking with Ranger Baird, who was making out the official incident report, when his phone rang. He checked the caller ID. The sight of the area code made his day.

Excusing himself for a moment, he walked a little distance off and clicked on. "Nicky? Is that you?"

"Yup. Thanks for the pictures."

"You're welcome. How about that one of us in front of the helicopter?"

"I love it! Hey, Vance? What are you doing?"

Vance's gaze took in the mile-long stream of vehicles passing the damaged school bus. The drivers kept stopping to get a look and take pictures, creating a monster traffic jam. He didn't know whether to laugh or cry. Since it was an impressionable, sensitive six-year-old he was talking to, he omitted the details and said, "Work."

Just work...

But even as he contemplated that thought, it shook him, because he'd never felt this way before. No matter what, he'd always experienced a certain joie de vivre in doing the kind of work he liked to do in the only place in the world he wanted to be. But something was missing since Nicky and his aunt had left.

A new kind of emptiness had set in. There was no antidote for what was wrong except to get them back to Yosemite. But in order for that to happen, she had to let go emotionally of Steven.

"I wish I could be there. Vance?" Nicky's voice was laced with regret.

Not immune to it, Vance gripped the phone tighter. "What is it, sport?" He asked the question, already knowing the answer.

"I wish Rachel and I hadn't had to leave. I want to be with you." Vance heard a sniffle, then a sob. Before long the boy was convulsed with tears.

In the background Rachel's father was urging him to hang up. Where was she? Vance wondered. With her ex? Nicky needed her *now*. And Vance needed to hear her voice.

"Come on, son," his grandfather prodded.

"Nooo! I don't want to get off! Please let me talk to Vance some more..."

"Nicky?" Vance called to him over the phone, anxious to try to smooth things over. But like the other day in Oakhurst, the child's emotions were out of control and he couldn't hear him. With every heartfelt cry, Vance's gut twisted a little more.

"Tell him goodbye," his grandmother finally said in a firm tone.

"O-kay. G-good-bye."

Vance heard another heaving sob, then a click.

This was agony. If he called Nicky back, that would make things so much worse. Yet it seemed criminal to do nothing. Either way, he was damned.

"Chief?" At the sound of Ranger Baird's voice, he jerked around. "Is the fire worse near Miguel Meadow?"

Fire? He shook his head to clear it. "No. It's been contained."

"That's good." The ranger appeared hesitant. "Are you all right?"

No, and I don't think I ever will be all right again. "Yes. Is your report finished?"

Baird nodded and handed it to him. Vance looked it over and signed it. "Excellent work."

"Thank you."

He handed it back. "I'm leaving for headquarters. Call me if you need me." The helicopter pilot stood by, ready to fly him back to the village.

Vance had interviews with two new rangers who'd transferred in from Zion National Park. After that he would be meeting the superintendent for lunch, on NPS business. Following that would be a four-hour seminar in the visitors' auditorium to discuss alternatives to prevent the spread of invasive plants into uninfested areas.

Vance wouldn't have to stay for all of it. At some

point he could slip out and phone Rachel, without Nicky being aware of it. They had to talk.

But as fate would have it, at the end of the day the park's chief biologist wanted a private conference with him. The night shift came on long before Vance's work was done and he could go home. Finally, he was off duty until morning. Chase would deal with any emergencies.

It had been a hot day. Vance was thirsty. Once inside the house he headed for the kitchen and bent down to drink cold water from the tap. But he needed something stronger.

His fridge offered beer and root beer. The latter he'd kept on hand in the event Nicky might end up at his house one last time. That had been wishful thinking. Vance grabbed a beer and slammed the door shut.

The clock in the kitchen said quarter to ten. It was quarter to one in Miami. Rachel would be in bed, unless she was out with her ex. Vance didn't want to think about what they might be doing.

After draining half the can, he moved into his den to look at the pictures he'd sent her and Nicky. Five minutes of that torture and he walked away from the computer. Until he could sleep, he needed to stay busy. Two months ago he'd promised himself he'd clean out his garage. It looked like tonight was the night.

He was twenty minutes into the project when his phone rang. He picked up. "Chief Rossiter speaking."

"Vance? It's Boyd."

He'd been expecting a call from the fire chief in Midpines, outside the park. "What's the status on the Telegraph fire?"

"That's why I'm calling. It's already burned sixteen thousand acres and it's only twenty percent contained.

El Portal's lost power. You'll be losing it in Yosemite Valley shortly."

He frowned. "What about Tuolumne Meadows?"

"Except for low visibility from smoke, no other areas of the park should be impacted."

"That's good news. Keep me posted."

"Will do."

There'd be no sleep for Vance tonight. The cleanup activity would have to keep for another day.

He switched off the garage light and went inside the house to change into his uniform. Once he'd turned on the outside generator, he headed for the visitor center. The smoke drifting their way from the Mariposa County fire was definitely getting heavier.

He nodded to the skeleton night crew manning the center. As he walked down the corridor past Chase's office, he saw him on the phone. Their eyes made contact. Chase covered the mouthpiece long enough to say, "Ranger Baird says the smoke from the Telegraph fire at the Arch Rock entrance has made driving dangerous."

"That's why I'm here. Boyd called me. The valley is the only place in the park that's going to lose power. Come on into my office. We'll make calls so the generators get turned on. All the tourist facilities first!"

Chase followed him down the hall. "While I'm at it, I'll give Wally and his crew a heads-up in case any of the generators need repair."

Vance raised his eyebrows. "What do you mean, 'in case'?"

His friend grunted before they both got to work.

RACHEL PULLED THE CAR UP in front of Blake's house. She turned to Nicky, who, even though he was wearing his Power Ranger costume, wasn't happy about anything. "I'll be back in two hours and I'll take you and Blake to get a hot dog for lunch."

"Promise?" That forlorn look on his face had been there since they'd returned from Yosemite a week ago. To her dismay Dr. Karsh had been out of town. She hadn't been able to talk to him until this morning. He'd told her to come in at ten.

"I promise."

"What are you going to do?"

"I'm looking for a new job." All last week she'd phoned about different positions in administration advertised in the paper and on the Internet. Today she had an interview at the Red Cross after her appointment with Dr. Karsh. "If you want to talk to Nana or Grandpa, just tell Blake's mom and she'll let you use the phone."

"Can't I phone you?"

"Yes, but I may be in an interview and not able to call you right back." Nothing she said seemed to reassure him. "Look, there's Blake. He's been waiting for you." The other boy came running toward them in his own Power Ranger costume.

Nicky slowly undid the restraint on his car seat and got out. The pained look in his eyes tore her apart. He'd had one nightmare since their return. Something had been flying at his head, and when he woke up screaming, he was calling out for Vance.

That dream had come the night they'd set up rules about phone calls to the chief ranger. Nicky could phone him once a week, that was all. Rachel had made Nicky tell Vance about the new rule within her hearing, but she herself had refrained from speaking to him.

Vance seemed to have taken his cue from that, because he'd only called Nicky once. For the six-year-old, two conversations in a week hadn't been enough for him.

"Don't forget your backpack. Your treats are in there."

He reached for it.

"I love you, darling."

His lower lip quivered as he shut the car door. She watched through the rearview window as she pulled away. Instead of running off with Blake, he stood looking after her until she'd driven out of sight.

Fifteen minutes later Rachel broke down in the doctor's office while telling him about their trip to Yosemite and the aftermath. He offered her a box of tissues.

"Thank you," she said, wiping the tears from her eyes and face. "To be honest, I don't know what to do. In some ways the situation seems worse than before."

"Not worse. Better," he commented.

"You're kidding…"

"No. What you said a minute ago is profound. Nicky does feel a very strong connection to the chief ranger because he was the last person to see his parents. But it goes deeper than that.

"This man tried to save them. He flew Nicky up to the top of El Capitan and showed him exactly where he searched for their bodies. When he found them, he made certain they were sent back to Florida. In Nicky's eyes, the ranger represents a father figure, someone who protects and takes care of everything, like Nicky's own dad once did.

"This connection isn't remarkable or unusual. It's totally understandable, given the fact that the chief ranger appears to be a remarkable man himself."

She nodded. "He's exceptional."

"That's why he's the chief." The doctor smiled. It made her smile. "As for the latest nightmare, it shows Nicky feels protected by him and likes it. That's a very good sign your nephew is capable of attaching himself to someone else besides his father. I'd say you're making progress, even though it doesn't feel that way yet."

"But how do I wean him from this latest attachment?"

"I'll know better after I've had a chat with Nicky. Could you bring him in at noon today?"

She was glad the doctor had a plan, because she was out of them. "Yes, of course."

After thanking him, she hurried from his office to the parking area. En route she canceled her interview at the Red Cross, then phoned Blake's mom and told her she'd be picking up Nicky sooner than planned. They would need to go home first so he could change out of his costume.

"You're home early," her dad said as she and Nicky walked into the dining room. His eyes darted to hers as he waited for an explanation. She would have told him, but her mother entered from the kitchen with a package in her hand.

"I'm glad you're back." Her gaze swerved to Nicky. "This came for you this morning."

He stared at it without much interest. "What is it?"

"I have no idea." Her mom was acting very mysterious. Rachel loved her for doing everything conceivable to help Nicky cope. "Want me to open it?"

"I can do it." He put it on the table and went to work, but couldn't remove the tape.

"Here." Her dad took a knife and made slits so Nicky could undo the flaps.

He reached inside and pulled out a plastic bag. After

a struggle he ripped it open and pulled out a Junior Park Ranger's uniform complete with shirt, shorts and a ranger's hat with the Yosemite logo.

"Whoa! Vance sent me a ranger's outfit!" he cried. "Now I can look just like him!"

Rachel's eyes closed tightly in reaction. He couldn't have picked out a gift that Nicky would love more, but he shouldn't have done it.

"I'm going to put it on. Rachel? Will you unzip the back of my costume?"

"Please?" her dad corrected him.

"Please. Sorry, Grandpa."

"Sure." Rachel's fingers were fairly trembling as she helped him peel off the red outfit and put on his new dark brown shorts with the light khaki shirt. They were a perfect fit.

Her mother picked up the card tucked in the bottom of the box and read it out loud. "'Dear Nicky, all the kids in the Junior Park Rangers Program sent you this present. Enjoy it. Ranger Cindy Davis.'"

What a darling thing for her to do.

"Let's see you in that hat." Ted opened it and put it on Nicky's head. "Well…don't you look official!"

Nicky beamed before hurrying into the bathroom to look at himself. When he came back, he opened the other box, which contained a pair of binoculars. There was a card with it, too. Rachel picked it up to read. "'To be used for owl watching. Have fun, sport.'"

Vance…

Nicky ran around the house trying out the binoculars. She heard shrieks of happiness. "Whoa—everything is huge! Whoa!"

Tears smarted Rachel's eyes. She wasn't the only

one moved by the moment. Soon he came running back into the dining room. "Look, Rachel!"

She took the binoculars from him and put them to her eyes, training them on her mother standing across the table from her. A gasp escaped her throat. The magnification was so powerful, at first Rachel wasn't sure what she was seeing. Finally she figured out it was one of her mom's eyelashes.

"Oh, Nicky, these are no ordinary children's binoculars. Vance sent you a very expensive, wonderful gift. You'll have to be extremely careful with them." She passed them to her father.

Once he put them to his eyes, he made sounds like Nicky had done. Ted quickly wheeled himself around to the entrance to the patio. "Do you know these are so powerful I can see a bumblebee's wing clear on the other side of the garden? Minnie, take a look."

Nicky ran over to them, waiting impatiently while his nana tried them out. Rachel hung back, still reacting to Vance's generosity. He had to know what this gift meant to her nephew. Considering that she had an appointment with Dr. Karsh to help keep Nicky from obsessing over the chief ranger, the timing was incredible.

She checked her watch. "Nicky?" By now he had the binoculars back in his possession. The gift would provide him hours of pleasure. "I have a doctor's appointment in a few minutes and am taking you with me." Her parents eyed her in surprise, because they thought she'd already been. "You'll need to change so we can get going."

"But I want to stay here and play."

"I know, but we have to go. Dr. Karsh wants to talk to both of us. It won't take a long time. Maybe later Blake can come over and see your new ranger outfit. Now run to your room and put on your T-rex shirt and shorts."

"But I don't want to change."

"Then wear that to the doctor's office," her mom suggested. She stared at Rachel as she said it, in the hope of preventing a confrontation.

"Can I, Rachel?"

She let out a troubled sigh. "Why not. But you'll have to leave the binoculars home. Give them to Grandpa."

"Okay."

Nicky gazed at his grandparents. "You can look through them if you want to. But you have to be very careful with them."

"Thank you," Minnie said with a straight face, although Rachel could see her mouth twitch ever so slightly. "We will."

Ted's chuckle followed them out the door.

On the way to the doctor's office Nicky said, "I want to call Vance." She'd been waiting for that. This was one time she couldn't say no, and Nicky knew it.

"Remember our rule. You can thank him when it's time."

"Can I send him a present?"

Her hands tightened on the steering wheel. She couldn't very well tell him no. "What did you have in mind?"

"A fly."

"I don't understand."

"He loves fishing more than anything!"

"Oh." In spite of the delicate situation, she couldn't help but smile. Who knew what other things he'd learned about his hero when they'd been gone all day looking for owls?

"It will have to be a very special fly."

"That's what he said. Most tourists use the wrong one."

"I bet Grandpa will know. He loves to fish, too."

"Yup."

Rachel glanced at her nephew in his ranger outfit and her heart melted. Dr. Karsh wouldn't believe how cute he was. When they entered his office a few minutes later, he took one look the boy, then flicked her a glance. "I thought you were bringing Nicky with you."

He giggled. "I'm Nicky."

After they sat down the doctor said, "Hmm. Take off your ranger hat." When Nicky complied, he said, "You got a haircut since the last time I saw you."

"Yup. Vance took me."

"Who's Vance?"

"He sent me this outfit in the mail today." Though the card had been written by Ranger Davis, Nicky knew Vance had been in charge. "Now we look alike."

"He sounds like a nice man."

"He's my best friend."

A smile broke out on the doctor's face. "Tell me about him."

"Vance can do anything. He's the chief ranger of the whole park."

"Did you like Yosemite?"

"Yes. He flew us on top of El Capitan, this huge rock where my mommy and daddy died. He put their bodies in the helicopter and sent them to my nana and grandpa."

"How did that make you feel?"

"Good. I love him. We went owl hunting and he showed me an old Indian trail. He said we could go visit the old Indian, Chief Sam, who's his friend. I wish our whole family lived there."

The doctor nodded. "My parents used to take me

to the mountains when I was your age. There was a mountain man I loved to visit named Jedediah. He used to show me all his stuff. He made his own ammunition and arrows. I wanted to live there, too, but I couldn't."

"How come?"

"Because my life was here in Miami. That's what's so great about vacations. You plan ahead so you have something exciting to look forward to. When it's time, you go and have a wonderful trip, then you come home and go to school and play with your friends until the next vacation, where you go and have a wonderful time all over again."

Dr. Karsh glanced at Rachel to see if she was getting the message. She got it. So did Nicky, who looked at her with pleading eyes. "Can we go to Yosemite on our next vacation?"

The doctor had come up with a clever plan to give Nicky hope while at the same time reducing his high level of anxiety. But it didn't take away hers. Another vacation to California meant seeing Vance again. She wasn't sure her heart could handle it.

"I think that's possible."

His eyes ignited with excitement. "When?"

"Do you know what, darling? Dr. Karsh has more patients to see. We'll talk about it when we get home."

"Okay."

The doctor walked them to the door. "Thanks for coming to see me, Nicky. I sure like your ranger outfit."

He put his hat back on. "Thanks. I love it."

Rachel smiled her thanks and they left to go out to the car. Anticipating Nicky's next question, she said, "We'll have to look at the calendar with Nana and Papa and see when we can arrange our next vacation, before your school starts. And then we have to check with Vance, because he goes on vacation, too."

Nicky's head jerked toward hers. "He does?"

"Of course. You heard Dr. Karsh. Everyone goes on vacations."

"Where does Vance go?"

"I don't know."

"I bet he goes to see Katy's headstone."

Rachel took an extra breath. "I'm sure he does that anyway." Was he still so much in love with her memory, he couldn't let another woman into his life? Rachel couldn't bear it if that was true.

"I'll ask him."

THE STUBBLE ON VANCE'S jaw felt like a week's growth instead of one night's worth. He was surprised his secretary didn't cry out in fright when she reported for work. With goodies no less. "How did you know to bring rations?"

She just laughed and put doughnuts and coffee in front of both him and Chase.

"You're an angel, Beth."

"How come my paycheck doesn't reflect it?"

"I don't know. We just work here."

Chase looked equally disreputable. "You're a sight for sore eyes this morning, Beth," he told her.

She peered into his. "Yours do look a little bloodshot."

"Thanks." He grinned. "What's it like breathing out there?"

"If you don't have asthma, you're okay."

Vance let out a sigh. "That's what I was afraid of. The superintendent isn't happy about it."

"Is he ever happy about anything?"

The two men looked at each other and shook their heads.

"The power at his house went out, too," Vance informed her. "Worse, someone had to go over to fix his generator. Luckily, we haven't had any complaints from the hotels or restaurants yet."

Chase finished off his third doughnut in two bites. "That has to constitute some kind of major miracle."

"From the looks of the two of you, I'd say you need to be in bed. Go on home. I'll call you if there's an emergency," she said as Vance's cell phone rang.

Through heavy lidded eyes he saw the Miami area code. His heart gave a clap before he clicked on. No doubt Nicky had received his present. He hoped to heaven Rachel was on the other end for once. The desire to hear her voice was turning into a burning need.

"Chief Rossiter speaking."

"Hi!"

That cute little voice. Vance grinned. "Hi, sport. How are you doing?" Chase's gaze darted to him with a smile. He knew who it was on the other end.

"Good. Thanks for the ranger outfit! I love it! I've got it on right now."

His smile widened. "Does it fit?"

"Rachel says it's perfect!"

So was she. "Tell her to take a picture of you in it and e-mail it to me."

"We already sent it. Vance? Thanks for the binoculars. They're awesome! This morning I could see an ant pulling a crumb from clear across the driveway! It didn't know I was looking."

While Vance was chuckling Nicky said, "When are you going on vacation?"

The question came as a surprise. He sat forward in his swivel chair. "I'm not taking one."

"How come? Dr. Karsh says everyone takes a vacation."

It sounded as if she and Nicky had been to the doctor. Vance needed to read between the lines here, but he didn't know exactly where this conversation was going.

"I agree with the doctor, but summer is the busiest time at the park, so I don't usually take one until later, when there aren't so many tourists."

"That's good, 'cause Rachel said I could have one more vacation before school starts. Can I come and visit you again? I want to see the whole park!"

Suddenly Vance's pulse was racing. "There's nothing I'd like better. When can you come?"

"Just a minute. Rachel wants to talk to you."

"Put her on." *Please.*

"Hello, Vance?" Her slightly breathless voice got to him every time.

"How are you?"

"We're better." That sounded like code. It meant Nicky wasn't quite as hysterical as the day he'd left to go back to Miami.

"I'm glad to hear it."

"Your gift meant more to him than all his Christmases put together."

It meant more to Vance to hear that than she could possibly imagine. "I'm looking forward to seeing his picture."

"I'm biased, of course, but it's so adorable he could be the Yosemite junior rangers' poster boy." She'd said it in a hushed tone.

"My secretary claims there's nothing like a male in uniform," Vance stated.

"Young or old, she's right."

Was that also code for something? He cleared his throat. "I'm at the office now. When I go home, I'll check my e-mail."

"You're up early, aren't you?"

"Actually, we've been here all night."

There was a brief pause. "I'm not surprised. It's been on the news about the you know what." He knew what she was talking about. With Nicky being right there, she had to choose her words carefully so as not to alarm him about the fire.

"It'll be contained in a few days, but we're okay. Just a lot of smoke. Thank heaven it didn't happen while you and Nicky were here."

"Thank heaven," she whispered. He felt the tremor in her voice.

"Nicky says you're coming out again before his school starts. The Fourth of July would be the best time for me." He didn't want to wait any longer to see them.

"That's less than two weeks away…"

Yup. The less she saw of her ex, the better. "High season at the park. Nicky will enjoy it."

Vance could practically hear her mulling things over. "I'd have to hurry to make reservations for everything."

"You take care of your flight arrangements and I'll provide you with a place to stay."

"But only if I pay for it."

"Agreed." He would agree to anything to get her back here. "Your room at the Yosemite Lodge will be waiting for you. Nicky said he wanted to see the whole park. That means you need to stay a week at least."

Chase gave him a thumbs-up.

"I—I'm not sure I can." Her voice faltered.

His jaw hardened. Was she back with her ex and didn't want to be gone that many days? Then another thought struck him. "Have you found a new job?"

"No. Not yet."

"Then there's no problem. Plan to come on the third. I'll pick you up at the Merced airport. Call me when you know your flight time."

"Vance—"

"Sorry," he said, purposely cutting her off. "I've got calls coming in on the other line. Tell Nicky I'll see him soon." He rang off before she could give him a reason why that date wouldn't work.

"I take it Rachel's coming back with Nicky," Chase said. "Did she mention her ex?"

"No. When I told Rachel she and Nicky could stay at the lodge the same as before, she didn't mention there'd be a third party with her. From what I gather, this trip is a form of therapy the psychiatrist has prescribed. I'm assuming he feels another vacation before school starts will help Nicky to settle down."

Chase squinted at him. "If you want my opinion, she can't wait to come back with Nicky."

Vance shot out of his chair, full of too many emotions and unanswered questions to sit there any longer. "I think maybe the psychiatrist has a lot to do with this. He may be thinking Nicky needs to come back right away to find out I didn't die like his parents."

In the next breath Chase stood up. Before he left the room he flashed Vance a speculative glance. "I think you're terrified."

Chase knew him too well. "I am," he admitted.

"Think of it this way. It could be a test to see if you've let Katy go." After that explosive salvo he let out a weary sigh. "Right now I'm going home to hit the sack."

Vance stood there in a shell-shocked daze. Damn if Chase hadn't connected with the jugular.

Rachel Lee

Then at least we'd be together, and not alone. Wouldn't that be better? Please believe me when I tell you it is your choice. Rena may try to make some kind of legal case now, and there are still other legal details to work out. Once I get your consent I'll be better prepared.

Chapter Eight

"Do you think Vance is waiting for us?"

Rachel clutched Nicky's hand tighter as they walked through the airline terminal to the baggage claim. "He said he'd meet us out front in a black Mazda."

Her nephew looked up at her with a solemn expression. She could barely see his eyes with his ranger hat on. "What if he's not there?"

"Then he'll phone us and tell us where he is."

"Oh, yeah." His face brightened.

After a few minutes Rachel saw their suitcase come up on the carousel, and she grabbed for it. "Let's go." She'd only brought one bag. After talking it over with her parents, she'd decided a five-day trip was all she could spare. So she hadn't packed either of them a lot of clothes.

Since she was still looking for work, she needed to nail down a job by the time Nicky's school started. At this point she wasn't even thinking career, just something to bring in a paycheck until Nicky was better equipped to handle life.

Rachel was running on faith where Dr. Karsh's advice was concerned. On the plane Nicky had asked her how soon they could plan their *next* vacation to Yosemite. She told him spring break.

He wanted to know how many days that made. In a burst of inspiration she'd suggested they count months instead. When she added them up, he said that was a long time to wait. But at least he didn't have hysterics. Of course, that was probably because he'd be seeing Vance within the hour.

That was all she'd been able to think about.

It had taken seeing Steven in her boss's office to realize the impact Vance Rossiter had made on her. When she'd called off her engagement, she hadn't been able to imagine caring about a man again. A year later she'd still been of the same mind. Then came the one quick trip to Yosemite for Nicky's mental health. After meeting Vance, she'd become a different person.

Rachel hoped enough time had passed that when she saw him in the next few minutes she'd be able to view him dispassionately—like an old family friend who was interested in Nicky's welfare. To read anything more into it could only bring her grief.

They headed out the sliding doors. "There's Vance!"

Nicky took off like a rocket. The tall, powerful-looking man waving to him stood next to his black car. He'd opened the front and back doors. Though dressed like an ordinary tourist in a pale blue sport shirt and khaki trousers, he appeared anything but. Rachel hurried forward, her heart thudding so fast she could hardly breathe.

"Hey, sport." After giving him a high five, Vance plucked him from the ground. While they exchanged a long, crushing hug, Nicky's ranger hat fell off. Rachel reached for it. As she straightened up she encountered a pair of blazing blue eyes focused on her. Their heat radiated to her core.

When he gave Nicky one more pat on the back before lowering him to the pavement, the sun reflected off Vance's gold wedding band. The reminder stopped her short.

"Welcome back," he murmured.

"It's wonderful to be here again," she replied without looking at him. "Thank you for picking us up."

Nicky had already climbed in the back, where a new car seat had been installed. He got right in it and fastened the strap. While Vance put their suitcase in the trunk, Rachel quickly got in the front seat so he wouldn't have to come around to help her.

"How come you're not wearing your uniform?" Nicky asked the second he slid behind the wheel.

Vance turned to look at him. "Because I'm on vacation."

His eyes widened. "You are?"

"Yup. For two whole days. I thought that as long as you're on vacation, too, we'd take them together over the Fourth of July. It's one of my favorite holidays."

"Hooray! Can we see the fireworks?"

"We're going to do it all."

Rachel struggled not to react in front of him. This wasn't part of the plan she'd envisioned, but in retrospect it would probably be easier on Vance, who knew Nicky needed his whole attention. Two days without having to continually worry about park business would be less frustrating for him.

That meant the other three days would have to be enjoyed without him at Nicky's beck and call. A shudder rocked her as she imagined Nicky having to share his hero for the latter part of their trip, but she wouldn't think about it right now.

"How does that sound to you?"

Feeling Vance's gaze leveled on her, she stirred restlessly. "Fantastic. We can't thank you enough for putting yourself out like this for us, can we, Nicky?"

"Nope. Are we going to light sparklers at your house?"

Vance still hadn't turned back around. His close proximity gave her this suffocating feeling in her chest. "The park doesn't allow fireworks of any kind because of fire danger, so we're going to celebrate in Oakhurst."

"Where your parents and grandparents are buried?"

"That's right. There'll be a big fireworks show tomorrow night."

"Goody!"

"I've got a motel for us right downtown, where we can walk around and play baseball at the local park. And later there's going to be a parade."

"Can we see it?" Nicky cried.

"We're going to be in it!"

Rachel's stunned gaze flew to his.

"We are?" chirped a joyous voice from the backseat.

"Yup. All the veterans in town will be riding on floats. You and Rachel can ride with me."

Her pulse sped up.

"What's a veteran?" Nicky asked.

"Anyone who served in the military. And after that there's going to be a town barbecue with all the corn on the cob and watermelon you can eat. In fact, they have a father and son contest to see which team can eat the most."

"I love watermelon. Can we be in it?"

"I'm planning on it." Vance's eyes sought Rachel's.

"Does all this meet with your approval?" he asked in a quiet voice.

He knew it did. Aside from family, who else but Vance realized just how much Nicky was missing his father? For two days he would play the part. Rachel loved him for it. "This will be a vacation he'll never forget," she whispered back.

Her answer seemed to satisfy Vance. "Everyone buckle up!"

"I already am!"

With a chuckle, he faced forward and started the car.

Rachel's excitement about being with him had escalated, because they would be away from the park. For a little while he'd be out of the spotlight, removed from everyone who knew him. It would probably be a relief for him to remain anonymous. She liked that aspect of it, too.

"Who's hungry?"

"I kind of am," Nicky said.

"Then we'll wait till we reach Oakhurst to eat a big meal."

"Can we get a root beer now?"

"That sounds good to me. How about you, Rachel?"

"Some root beer with ice cream would be yummy."

Once they left the airport, it didn't take Vance long to find a drive-through. They ended up buying root beer floats. From then on Nicky entertained them with his chatter until they reached Oakhurst.

Vance checked them into the two-story motel on the main street near the local park. He drove them down to a unit and parked the car in front. They had rooms side by side bordering the swimming pool. Nicky was ecstatic. He ran back and forth between the sliding doors while she and Vance settled in with their luggage.

The pool management had a selection of water toys guaranteed to keep children entertained. Since it had been a long flight from Miami, they decided to go out for a meal, then come back and play in the pool until time for bed. Tomorrow would be a big day. It was decided they all needed a good night's sleep.

After a quick shower, Rachel changed into a sleeveless, jewel-green blouse and white wraparound skirt that tied at the side of her waist. She'd bought the outfit and a pair of white sandals for the trip. Once she'd brushed her layered hair and put on pink frost lipstick, she was ready.

Nicky and Vance stood outside by the car waiting for her. When she walked toward them, she felt a pair of intense blue eyes flick over her in male appreciation, but she refused to let herself read anything deeper into it. The fact that Vance hadn't taken off his ring meant he truly was here for Nicky's sake and no other reason. After the tragic accident that had deprived Nicky of his parents, it was his way of assuaging needless guilt.

A secret part of her had hoped he wanted to get to know her better this trip, and might show up without it. After all, the possibility of them being together again in the future like this was pretty remote, even considering Nicky's mental health. Yet knowing that, Vance wasn't moved to take their relationship any further.

Since he was prepared to play fill-in father for the next few days, she would pretend he was her long-lost brother. That way she just might make it through this torture, because there was no other adjective to describe her emotions right now.

Maybe another woman wouldn't let a ring deter her from pursuing the man she wanted, but Rachel's experience with Steven had taught her not to go there. The woman he'd been involved with before Rachel had a much greater hold on him than even he had imagined. Otherwise he wouldn't have slept with Lynette on the eve of his marriage to someone else.

If Vance hadn't been able to let go of Katy after five years, no woman stood a chance against her memory. Anyone who tried would be deluding herself at her own peril. But there was just one problem. Rachel had already fallen in love with Vance. Her feelings for him couldn't be undone.

"There's a mall we can walk to a block from here, with all kinds of places to eat. What do you feel like?"

"Shall we wait till we get there and then decide what Spiderman wants?" Rachel suggested, smiling at Nicky, who'd finally changed out of his ranger outfit into his Spiderman shirt and shorts.

"I don't think any of the restaurants serve flies," Vance said, poker-faced.

"Rachel!" Nicky suddenly cried. "I've got to go back in the room for a minute!" He broke away from them.

"Wait…" she called after him. "Can't we do it later?" He'd just used the bathroom.

He flashed her a frustrated look before running back to whisper in her ear, "I want to give Vance his present."

Oh—the *present*.

"Excuse us for a minute, Vance." She pulled the card key from her purse to open the door. Nicky ran inside, grabbed the small gift-wrapped package off the dresser and dashed back out. Rachel shut the door and joined them.

"This is for you."

"How come?" Vance took it from him.

"'Cause I wanted to."

"Well, that's the best reason in the whole world to give someone a gift." He smiled down at Nicky, who was beaming.

"Aren't you going to open it?"

"Right now?"

He nodded. Vance put it up to his ear and shook it.

Nicky laughed. "It can't make noise."

"You're right. I didn't hear a sound in there. Are you teasing me about something being inside?"

"Nope."

In two seconds Vance had unwrapped it and opened the box. Two flies lay inside. He lifted them out. "A pale morning dun and a blue wing olive? Now *these* are how you catch Sierra trout! This is the best present anyone ever gave me!"

"Grandpa helped me."

"Well, he surely knows his stuff. Rachel, do you mind?" He put everything in her hands before picking Nicky up to give him a huge hug. He swung him around. "We'll have to test these out when we go hiking in a couple of days."

"Yeah!"

"I've got the perfect fishing pole for you. My grandpa gave it to me. I've caught more fish on it than any other."

They started walking. Rachel brought up the rear. She put everything in her purse, but didn't try to get a word in. Vance was telling Nicky an outrageous fish tale. Her nephew was taking it all in with a look of pure wonder on his precious face. The moment was so tender, she could hardly see for the moisture glazing her eyes.

VANCE MADE CERTAIN their motel room was locked up tight before he said good-night and left for his own.

Once Nicky had settled down and said his prayers, Vance had no more excuse to stay.

As he put the box of flies on the dresser, his glance fell on his hand. Katy's ring glinted up at him. There was no use fooling himself any longer. He'd wanted to remove it since the night he'd taken Rachel to his house for dinner, but the fear that she and Steven had resumed their relationship after she'd gone back to Miami prevented him from doing it.

No poaching on another man's preserves. That was the unwritten law Vance's grandfather had taught him. It didn't matter that she'd broken off with the guy a year ago. If she still had feelings for him deep down, then Vance didn't have a prayer with her.

Though she'd been charming and friendly to him since he'd picked them up at the airport, she hadn't said or done anything to let him know where things stood with Steven.

Unfortunately, if her feelings for her ex were dead, Vance still wouldn't know it, not while he was wearing Katy's ring. Chase had been right about that. Rachel wasn't the kind of woman who presumed anything. That was one of the traits he found so unique and appealing about her.

He sank down on the side of the bed with his hands clasped between his legs. It was a mess. What to do?

What do you want to do, Rossiter?

If she saw it was gone from his finger in the morning, would it make a difference in how she responded to him? Would she ask him about it?

She'd never initiated conversation about Katy. And what if she didn't? What if she didn't care? What then?

The thing he'd thought would never happen, had happened! He was madly in love for the second time in his life. How would he handle it if she didn't love him back with the same intensity? The answer terrified him, just as Chase had said.

Nicky was the only constant in the equation. Vance would love him like a son till the day he died.

THE FOURTH HAD BEEN A DAY of enchantment for Nicky, starting with breakfast and a baseball game at the park. However, Rachel drew the line at riding on the float. She insisted on following them from the sidewalk while she took pictures with her video camera.

Nicky wore his park ranger outfit and held an American flag. Vance wore his dress blues complete with white cap and gloves. In the midnight-blue uniform with the sky-blue trousers, he stood out from the dozen military men representing all the branches of the Armed Forces riding the same float.

She couldn't count the number of times she heard some woman say, "Look at that marine—he's drop-dead gorgeous!" Rachel's thoughts exactly.

People lining the streets clapped when they drove by. Nicky was in heaven. He stood straight at Vance's side. Once in a while he flashed her a smile and waved. There were a lot of floats with servicemen and patriotic music. It brought a lump to her throat. Her father would love this video. Rachel would treasure it forever.

After the parade, they went back to the motel to change and get ready for the barbecue. When it came to the watermelon-eating contest, Nicky's eyes were bigger than his stomach. After two pieces he had to quit.

Vance laughed. "It's okay, sport. I don't have room, either. Let's go get us a good place on the bleachers to watch the fireworks."

The park had been filling fast. By the time they found a spot, they had to wedge themselves in. Rachel ended up sitting between Nicky and a woman who had a daughter about his age sitting in front of her. Darla, the little girl, was so outgoing she told Nicky to sit with her, and made room for him. Talk about hilarious.

"Is it okay?" he asked Vance instead of Rachel. That's when she knew the bonding between the two males was complete.

"Sure. You can share your popcorn with her."

As soon as Nicky moved down, Vance shifted closer to Rachel. The contact spread warmth through her body. Now that it was night, she could hardly see the color of his eyes, but she felt their heat. "This is nice," he murmured near her ear. "Everyone has someone."

Rachel wanted to throw herself in his arms. Instead she said, "Thank you for making this a perfect day, Vance. Nicky will never forget it."

For some reason her response seemed to create tension. After a slight pause he said, "It's not over yet."

Suddenly rockets exploded in the night sky. Rachel felt them bursting inside of her. The display drew oohs and aahs from the crowd, Nicky's and Darla's the loudest. For the next half hour they all enjoyed the show.

On the walk home after the grand finale, Nicky regaled them with news about Darla's pug, Mitzi, who had to stay indoors in the basement because she got scared by the fireworks. That brought up a whole other conversation, about Vance's mutt who'd died before he'd gone to college.

Samson was buried in the backyard instead of the cemetery. Nicky wanted to know if his grave had a headstone. Vance told him it had a wood marker, and promised to show it to him before they left Oakhurst for the park.

By the time Nicky had brushed his teeth and put on his Ninja Turtle jammies, he was so tired he didn't need a story. Once he'd said his prayers, he was out for the count.

Vance kissed his forehead before turning to Rachel.

"It's a beautiful night. Let's sit out by the pool for a little while. We'll keep the sliding door open in case Nicky wakes up."

Rachel had never been so tempted, but she didn't dare. Her feelings for Vance were too raw for her to be alone with him right now. During the fireworks show she'd made a decision about something, and was going to stick by it no matter how badly it was going to upset Nicky.

"Much as I'd like that, it's late, Vance. You have to get back to the park tomorrow."

His brows furrowed. "We're all going to the park in the morning."

"No." She shook her head and backed away from him. "A day like today can never be repeated. Nicky's had the perfect vacation with you. Tomorrow I'm going to rent a car and take him to Sequoia Park. As long as we're in California, I want him to see as much as he can before we return to Miami."

She felt Vance's body stiffen. "Why would you do that? You've only seen a tiny portion of Yosemite."

The tension between them was palpable. "You have a park to run. We've already imposed too much on your time as it is."

"What's this all about, Rachel?" He sounded really angry.

She rubbed her palms against her hips, a gesture he followed with his eyes. "Why are you so upset?" she asked.

"Why do you think?" he retorted. "For one thing, I

had plans for all of us to go hiking. For you to suddenly change the itinerary isn't fair."

She raised a hand to her throat. "I—I'm sorry."

He headed for the front door and opened it before pausing. The outside light threw his profile into stony relief. "You never mentioned visiting Sequoia on the phone. Admit it's just an excuse. If you're so anxious to get back to Steven, don't use my job as the reason you've decided you can't stay here any longer. Nicky deserves to know the truth, don't you think? He's already been put through enough trauma by not understanding all the facts a year ago."

To her shock he shut the door, leaving his words hovering in the air like sparks from a live wire.

Without conscious thought she ran over and flung it open. "Vance?" she called as he was opening the door to his room. He glanced in her direction, key in hand. She'd had no idea he could look so forbidding. This was worse than the first time they'd spoken to each other, in his office.

"Please come back," she urged him.

She heard his sharp intake of breath. "I don't think it would be a good idea."

"Just come over here to the door for a minute. If we're quiet, we won't wake Nicky."

"I prefer not to have a discussion in front of an audience."

He had a point. People had been returning to the motel, catching her and Vance in the headlights of their vehicles.

"Then we'll go out on the patio as you suggested."

"You were right the first time. It's late."

Leaving the door ajar, she closed the distance between them. "I had no idea what I said would make you angry."

Vance stood there rubbing the back of his neck. "I apologize for that. Nicky has come to mean a lot to me."

"He *loves* you." Her voice throbbed.

"In retrospect, I can understand why you don't want to stay at Yosemite any longer. After you return home to Steven, Nicky's going to be difficult again."

She sucked in her breath. "You're right."

Vance lifted his head. "Does Steven love Nicky?"

"No. Steven only loves himself. While I was dating him, Nicky lived with his parents and wasn't around him that much. But it's irrelevant, because it's over with Steven."

"That isn't what Chase told me."

His comment took her by surprise. Apparently there were no secrets between the two men. "I did tell Chase I was going back to explore my true feelings for him."

"So what happened?"

She drew in another deep breath. "I discovered they're dead. Steven killed them a long time ago."

The silence between them grew.

"You mean it's really over with him?"

"Yes. I saw him at the cruise line office when I turned in my resignation. It meant nothing to me."

"Did you tell him that?"

"Yes."

"Did he accept it?"

"No, but that's his pride talking."

Vance studied her intently. "If you're not running home to him, then why aren't you planning to spend the rest of your trip at Yosemite? That was the doctor's prescription, wasn't it? Let Nicky think this was the first of many vacations out here, to calm his problem of separation anxiety?"

Rachel eyed him in awe. "You're very discerning, Vance. That's exactly what he had in mind. It works well in theory."

Lines darkened his features. "It has worked out extremely well in reality. I don't understand the problem."

"You're the chief ranger. I can't ask you to drop your responsibilities at a moment's notice for Nicky, no matter how willing you might be. Please don't fight me on this," she begged, sensing he was going to argue with her. "We've had a fantastic two days. To expect more interferes with your job.

"If my family lived in California and I could drive Nicky to the village to see you for a couple of hours once in a while at your convenience, that would be one thing. But we live thousands of miles away.

"After I get a job, it will be even more difficult to plan vacation times. When we can come, you might not be available. I hate the idea that you have to drop everything to accommodate us. It isn't right and I won't put you through it."

He stared hard at her. "I've already suggested another solution. While I'm at work tomorrow, why don't you report to the park's human resources office and fill out the application for that job I offered you? Sleep on it, and we'll talk about it in the morning."

Her mind reeled. He really expected her to sleep? What he'd offered was a temporary solution to Nicky's problem, but there was no guarantee that Vance would always work at the park. No guarantee that he'd remain single, when he was ready for another woman in his life.

To live close to him, to work for him, to *almost* have a life with him... Rachel couldn't put herself or

Nicky through that. She didn't want a job unless it was being his wife!

She wanted the right to be under his roof with him 24-7, in his arms, in his bed. Rachel wanted a baby with him. Nothing short of that would do.

By next spring she would make certain they were in another place psychologically and emotionally, because she had no intention of coming to Yosemite again.

"You're a very generous, thoughtful man, but I don't need to sleep on it. My life is back in Miami with my parents and Nicky. He's going to be all right, I *know* he is. However, since you've made plans for us over the next few days, I don't want to disappoint you or Nicky, so we'll see you in the morning. Good night."

She went back to her motel room. After shutting the door, she leaned against it and sobbed. Two more days before she and Nicky were gone, then the chief ranger would finally be able to put this episode behind him and get on with *his* life.

Chapter Nine

Vance had set his alarm for seven-thirty, but was already awake at six-thirty when the call came through on his cell. It was from Chase, who'd been in charge while Vance was gone.

He threw off the covers and sat up. Putting the phone to his ear, he said, "Happy fifth of July, Chase. Is the park still there?" It was one of their little jokes whenever one of them had been away.

"You'll never guess what an ill wind has blown in."

His reply, blurted without preamble, coincided with Vance's raw mood. Chase was right; he couldn't guess. Unless it was the superintendent with a host of outspoken VIPs wanting to be entertained.

"Steven's here. He called headquarters from the Ahwahnee, wanting to know where to find Rachel. Apparently he phoned Nicky and found out they were coming here for the Fourth."

Vance sprang to his feet. "I can't say I'm surprised. Last night Rachel told me it was over with him, but she said he refused to accept that. I'll tell her after we get to the park, so she's prepared."

There was an eloquent pause before Chase said, "Sounds to me like you were given the green light last night."

His hand tightened on the phone. "Let's just say a big obstacle has been removed. Now I've got to work on finding out how she feels about me."

"Then you know what you've got to do."

Vance glanced at the ring on his finger. Yup. He knew. But he'd wait until she got rid of Steven first. He needed to see it happen with his own eyes.

"Once I've dropped them off at the Yosemite Lodge, I should be in the office by eleven. Is there any park business to report?"

"You'll be glad to know the Telegraph fire has been fully contained."

"That'll make breathing a lot easier. Just so *you* know, when I return you're to go off duty for the next twenty-four hours so you can catch up on your sleep. See you soon."

He hung up and headed for the shower. As he stepped out of the stall a few minutes later, he heard a knock on the sliding glass door. "Vance? Can I come in?"

Nicky always brought a smile to his face. Today he was back in his ranger outfit. Vance hitched a towel around his hips and let him in, automatically picking him up and giving him a hug. Nicky rewarded him with a huge hug back.

"How did you sleep?"

"Great. Can I watch you shave?"

Vance chuckled. "Sure you can. Come on in the bathroom."

"How come girls don't have to?"

He lathered his jaws and began to make inroads

with the razor. "You mean Rachel doesn't have a beard?" he teased.

Nicky laughed. "No."

"Aren't we glad?"

"Yeah." He watched with great interest. "Do you have to go to work today?"

"Yes, but when I'm through, we'll eat dinner at my house and light off snakes."

"Real snakes?" He looked worried.

"No." Vance rubbed the boy's head. "They look like little black nibs. You light them and they grow and then break apart like ashes in a fireplace. I always do some on the Fourth of July, but we couldn't light them here at the motel. You need a piece of wood. After it's too dark to see them, we'll watch *Spiderman*. How does that sound?"

"Hooray!"

Nicky followed him into the other room. They could hear Rachel calling. He ran over to the sliding door and poked his head out. "I'm in here. Vance is up. Come on in!"

When she stepped inside, wearing jeans and a peach-colored top, Vance was pulling his uniform from the closet. He felt her gaze sweep over him, dressed as he was in his towel, and liked the feeling.

"Oh!" she cried in embarrassment. Her cheeks filled with color. "I'm sorry. I thought—"

"Nicky knows I'm decent," he murmured, and went into the bathroom to get dressed. When he came out, naturally they'd gone.

He looked around the motel room, cluttered as it was with the water toys, a balloon, candy wrappers, soda cans, fishing flies, clothes, towels, Nicky's *Dumb*

Bunnies book, a Bible the boy had found in the drawer. All evidence of a family trip.

For so many years Vance had forgotten what that was like. The only things missing were a lacy nightgown lying in a pool at the side of the bed, a lipstick with the top off, a bikini hanging in the bathroom to dry. He'd loved the past eighteen hours so much he ached inside, unable to bear that it couldn't continue.

WITH A FEELING OF DÉJÀ VU, Rachel began unpacking in the VIP suite of the Yosemite Lodge she and Nicky had occupied before. While he'd stopped to look at the owl mural in the foyer, Vance had dropped his bombshell. Steven was here looking for her? Apparently Chase had phoned Vance with the news.

It didn't surprise her Steven would go this far. All she felt was disgust. "Nicky? Did Steven happen to call the house the other day?"

"Yup. I told him you were out shopping for our trip." He looked a little nervous. "I forgot to tell you. Are you mad?"

"Of course not. I don't love him anymore and I don't want him to phone me ever again."

"Grandma and Grandpa said he hurt you. You're not going to marry him, huh."

"Absolutely not."

"Why is he here?"

"He came to the park to try to get me to like him again, but I can't."

"I'm glad."

"We'll probably have to talk to him for a minute before he goes back to Miami, but I don't want you to be worried about it."

"I'm not. Vance is here. He'll make him leave, like he did those mean guys at the pool."

"Yeah…" Rachel loved that idea. Steven wouldn't stand a chance against the chief ranger.

Nicky let out a little sigh. "I wish Vance didn't have to go to work today."

If she counted every "I wish" Nicky had said since the first night he'd met Vance in June, those words would circle the world end to end.

Spoiled rotten. That's what the chief ranger had done to both of them.

"I wish I had a dog. Vance loved Samson so much he buried him under that big tree in his backyard. He told me he saw a cemetery in France that's just for dogs."

"I've heard of it."

"How come we don't do that here?"

"Maybe we do."

"If I lived with Vance he'd let me have a dog."

"Papa would let you have one if he weren't allergic to everything. You know what? We need to call your grandparents. They'll be up eating breakfast by now."

"Yeah. I'm going to tell Papa Vance loved the flies! We're going hiking and fishing tomorrow. After we get back he says we're going to have a fish fry. Do you like trout?"

"I love it."

"Vance says we're going to *really* love it 'cause he has this special way to cook it. He filluts it."

"You mean 'fillet.'"

"What does that mean?"

"You take out all the bones first."

"Is that hard to do?"

"Not when you know how."

"Vance knows how to do everything."

"You're right."

"I want to stay here forever."

"I know." She put the last stack of clothes in the drawer and carried the empty suitcase to the closet.

Vance had offered her a job that could make Nicky's dream come true. If her parents weren't alive, she might consider it, even knowing the risk of permanent heartache. But there was no way she could leave them. They needed her and Nicky too much.

"I told Vance I miss my mommy."

That comment took her breath away. He rarely talked about Michelle. Dr. Karsh said he would when the time was right. Rachel sank down on the side of the bed. "What did he say?"

Nicky wandered over to her and stood in front of her. "He said he misses his mommy, too, but we don't need to worry 'cause they're watching over us from heaven."

Her eyes stung from tears she was fighting. "I know they are, darling. You and Vance are their boys. They love you more than anything in the whole world."

He looked into her eyes. "You love me more than anything, huh."

"More than anything!" she cried, before pulling him into her arms.

"I love you more than anything. I love Nana and Papa, too."

A new Nicky was emerging. Rachel knew exactly who to thank for this miracle. She wiped her eyes. "Let's get them on the phone so you can tell them that."

She got up and reached for her cell on the dresser. After she punched the number she handed it to Nicky. This call was going to make their day. Since he would keep them riveted for at least ten minutes, she picked up the phone by the bed and rang the Ahwahnee Hotel.

It was the most famous and expensive place to stay at the park. In the brochure she'd read that the historic landmark had thirty-five-foot ceilings, full-length stained glass windows, giant stone fireplaces, massive hand-stenciled beams and rich tapestries. Some U.S. presidents had stayed there, even the Queen of England. She and Nicky had plans to explore it, but not while her ex-fiancé was staying there.

After leaving a message for Mr. Steven Dunmore, she hung up and gave her attention to Nicky, who was still recounting yesterday's adventures to her parents.

Finally he handed the phone to her. "They want to talk to you."

"Hi, you two."

"Oh, Rachel, honey. He sounds like our old Nicky," her mom said.

"I know." Vance was responsible. "You should have seen him on that float with Vance, both of them in uniform. I can't wait to show you the video! You're especially going to love it, Dad."

Rachel couldn't wait to see it on a big screen. During the long hours of the night she'd replayed the footage on the camera. She needed to get it on disk in case something went wrong with the camcorder.

After more tears and laughter they hung up. Rachel patted Nicky's shoulder. "Let's go downstairs and eat lunch. Steven might come while we're eating. Maybe not. It doesn't matter. We'll go swimming after."

"Goody. I want to float with my new water wings."

As she reached for her purse, the hotel phone rang.

Steven didn't waste any time. Steeling herself to be civil in front of Nicky, she picked up. "Hello?"

"Rachel? It's Chase Jarvis."

"Oh—Chase, how are you?"

"Good. I understand Nicky had a great Fourth."

"It was the best, but I'm sorry to hear my ex-fiancé showed up to bother you."

"It was no problem. I understand he's still your ex and going to remain that way."

Since she'd told Chase she was going back to Miami to explore her feelings for Steven, evidently there were no secrets at this point. "As I explained to Vance, it's definitely over. Nicky and I were just on our way downstairs to the dining room. If you're free, please feel welcome to join us." In a short amount of time Chase had become a good friend.

"I'll be there in ten minutes."

After he rang off she turned to Nicky, who'd put on his new cowboy hat. They'd bought identical hats and had walked all around downtown Oakhurst like cowboys who'd ridden in for the day. Nicky had enjoyed his first bottle of old-fashioned sarsaparilla, a form of root beer. He'd been in heaven. So had she.

"Do you remember Ranger Jarvis?"

He nodded while he tried to pop his balloon.

"He's going to eat lunch with us."

"How come?"

"Because I asked him. Do me a favor and don't talk about Vance all the time."

"Why?"

"Because as you said, Vance can do everything bigger and better and greater than anyone else. It could make Ranger Jarvis feel bad. He and Vance are best friends."

"But *I'm* Vance's best friend."

"Besides you."

"Oh. Okay."

"Leave the balloon here."

"Can I wear my gun belt?"

"If you don't shoot off any caps. Now let's go."

He fastened the buckle and they left the room. She'd bought him a pair of cowboy boots, too. The spurs jingled as he walked. No sooner did they reach the entrance to the dining room than she heard a familiar voice behind her say, "Wait up, Rachel."

She turned around to see Steven walking toward her. Nicky automatically reached for her hand. "You have an amazing amount of nerve," she said in a low voice. "First you show up in Harry's office uninvited, now here."

His eyes glittered. "You're a cool customer, you know that? You act like I'm an alien."

"In a way you are, because you're not the man I thought you were." She started walking to an empty table. He followed and sat down with them. His gaze swerved to Nicky.

"Hi, Tex."

"I'm Roy!"

Rachel started to laugh. She couldn't help it. At the pool in Oakhurst, Vance had pretended to be the bad guy chasing Roy Rogers.

"What's so damn funny?" Steven demanded.

"Please don't swear." The minute the words came out, Chase came into view, wearing his uniform. His keen gray gaze surveyed the scene before he walked up to the table and sat down.

After removing his hat he smiled at her. "Hi!"

"Hi yourself."

Steven scowled and turned to Nicky. "Hey, Roy. This must be your sidekick."

Things were unraveling fast. Rachel spoke up. "Chase Jarvis, this is Steven Dunmore from New World Cruise Lines in Miami. Chase is the assistant head ranger of the park."

Chase nodded, but Steven just sat there staring bullets.

The waitress chose that moment to come over and take their orders. Rachel and Nicky both picked chicken quesadillas and lemonade. Chase said he would have the same thing. Steven ignored their server.

Once the waitress left he said, "I'd like to see you alone."

Rachel shook her head. "We have nothing to say to each other. I wish you'd go."

"Harry's still holding your job open for you."

"Rachel's not going on any more cruises," Nicky piped up, bless his little heart. "She promised."

She patted his hand. "That's right, darling."

"How are you going to keep up those high payments on your condo? A salary like yours doesn't come along every day. Without me you wouldn't have gotten that last promotion."

He was lying, but she refused to rise to the bait. Even for Steven he'd sunk to a new low. What on earth had she seen in him?

"Are you through?"

"Smoky the Bear here doesn't make beans in comparison."

He was out of control. She couldn't believe it. "You sound like a ten-year-old, Steven, and growing younger by the minute."

A ruddy color entered his cheeks. "You're going to be sorry you walked away from me."

"I've had a year to find out if I was sorry. It never happened. You're only digging yourself into a deeper hole. I'm busy right now. Do you mind?"

"What if I do?" he challenged. "I flew clear across the country to talk to you."

"No one asked you to come."

"Rachel—"

"The lady wants you to leave," Chase said.

Steven's eyes flashed in anger. "Butt out!"

Chase calmly pulled the cell from his pocket to phone security. When Steven realized what was happening, he shot out of the chair, livid. "You two are welcome to each other!"

On his way out of the dining room he narrowly missed the waitress bringing their food. Rachel couldn't believe what a boy he was. She was embarrassed to think she'd almost married him.

While they ate, a couple of rangers came over to Chase. After he had a brief word with them, they took off, no doubt to make certain Steven didn't cause any trouble.

Chase turned to her. "Are you all right?"

"Yes, thanks to you."

"Steven was mad, huh," Nicky said.

"Yes, but he'll get over it once he's home."

"I'm going to tell Vance," the boy announced before taking another bite of food.

Rachel had been waiting for him to bring up Vance's name. He couldn't help it. She tucked into her own lunch with gusto.

"What are your plans for this afternoon?" Chase asked.

"We're going to swim," she told him. "What about you?"

"I've got business to take care of. Now that Steven's gone, I hope you two will enjoy yourselves at the pool. It sounds fun."

"Thanks, Chase. You know what I mean." Vance had probably asked him to run interference in case there was trouble.

"You bet." He got up from the table. "I'll see you around, Roy."

"See ya."

He put on his hat and nodded to her before striding away.

"Can we go get our swimsuits on now?"

"Have you finished everything?"

"Yup."

"Okay."

THREE FEDERAL AGENTS accompanied Vance to the region above Porcupine Creek. One of them whistled to see a carpet of spiky marijuana plants covering the area. "There must be fifty thousand at least."

Vance nodded. "Add the plants I found in the Tuolumne Meadows in June and we're talking three hundred thousand, maybe more. This is hardly the sight John Muir described when he first came through here."

The famous Scotsman had worried the alpine meadows wouldn't survive the twentieth century. Vance loved the area, too. It was beautiful, like a garden of flowers thriving at the high elevations.

Tomorrow Vance yearned to show Rachel and Nicky this divine spot, even with its evidence of mankind's encroachment.

"Two weeks ago we confiscated a thousand pounds of fertilizer and at least twenty weapons," he informed the other men. "I've hauled twelve suspects into custody so far. Ranger Jarvis will be heading up a team on horseback to search for the rest."

"We'll get our people out here in the morning. The state is sending in aircraft for an aerial view."

"Anything else my office can do to assist, just let me know."

"You and the chief ranger over at Sequoia have done more to help in this effort than everyone else put together. Thank you, Vance."

They shook hands before making their way back to the helicopter, where Perry was waiting for them. It was 5:30 p.m. Once they returned to the village, Vance would be off duty. With Mark taking over, Vance would have the rest of the evening to entertain Rachel and Nicky. He'd been living for that moment.

En route Ranger Baird called him on his cell. "Chief Rossiter here. What's up?"

"There was a van rollover near White Wolf Campground, a family of six. The area's been cordoned off. Aid is being given at the scene. We've sent for Air Life Rescue support."

"Any known fatalities?"

"No, sir. For once everyone was wearing a seat belt, but the mother is seven months pregnant."

Vance closed his eyes. "Keep me posted."

"Will do."

Before the chopper landed he had another call. He picked up. "This is the chief."

"It's Ranger Thompson. There's been a car fire two miles north of Wawona. It has burned through the shrubs lining the highway for close to a half acre, but should be contained any minute now."

"Anyone hurt?"

"No, sir. We're doing one-way traffic until the fire chief gets things cleared off."

"Keep a watch in case any sparks drift."

"We're already on it."

"I'll be back at headquarters in ten minutes. Give me another update then."

"Yes, sir."

Sometimes trouble came in threes. Instinct told him there'd be another call before he hurried over to the lodge to collect Rachel and Nicky. He was almost breathless thinking about them.

After leaving the military to become a ranger, how had he lived and functioned every day without them?

As they neared Yosemite Village, Perry got on the speaker. "Chief? Ranger Sims wants you to know a 4.3 magnitude earthquake hit the Mammoth Lakes area a few minutes ago and was felt strongly at headquarters."

That was over sixty miles away. "Any collateral damage reported from the hotels yet?"

"He's still assessing. Every ranger's expected to call in, but he said there was a lot of rattling."

Vance broke out in a cold sweat. Rattling was all Nicky needed to be terrified. There could be aftershocks. He'd never want to visit the park again. This was one time Vance was thankful Chase was with them. No one kept a cooler head in a crisis than his friend.

Stuck in the air until they landed, he phoned Chase, who picked up on the second ring. "Vance? I take it you've heard the news."

"I'm still in the air, coming back from Porcupine

Creek. Perry just got the word from Mark. How are Nicky and Rachel?" His voice shook. He needed to talk to them and reassure Nicky.

"I don't know."

He clutched the phone tighter. "What do you mean? I thought you'd be with them."

"I joined her and Nicky for lunch. Steven was there. She told him to leave, that it was over for good. When he refused, I called security and he took off. He won't be back, Vance. After that I left, because Nicky didn't want to do anything with me. He made it clear he and Rachel were going swimming. That's all I know."

Vance couldn't have heard better news, but he needed to know if Rachel and Nicky were all right now. "Are you home?"

"No. I went horseback riding with a couple of the guys, to check fishing permits. The minute we got the call from headquarters I phoned Rachel, but her voice mail was on. We're checking campgrounds now on our way back. I should be there within a half hour."

"Did you feel any tremors?"

"Nothing, but I would imagine Nicky was scared out of his wits. California's not Florida. This isn't going to help his nightmares any. Rachel's, either."

Vance's thoughts exactly. "You're right." He took an extra breath. "We're about to set down. I'll stay in close touch."

The second he hung up he called Rachel's cell phone. Adrenaline was rushing through him. *Pick up.*

"Rachel?" he cried when she answered after the first ring.

"Oh, thank God, Vance…"

She took the words out of his mouth. The concern in

her voice was gratifying, to say the least. "How are you and Nicky?"

"We're fine now that I'm talking to you."

"Where are you?"

"At headquarters, in Beth's office."

His heart couldn't take much more. "What are you doing there?"

"We'd just finished swimming, and Nicky was in the tub when everything started to shake. It didn't last very long and nothing broke, but it made the water swish back and forth. That's when I realized we'd just felt our first earthquake.

"Nicky looked at me for an explanation. When I told him, he climbed out of the tub determined to find you and make sure you were all right. We both got dressed and hurried over to your office. He wasn't frightened until he found out you were somewhere else in the park and might be hurt. H-he loves you so much, Vance."

Tears stung his eyes. When he could swallow again he said, "Put him on, will you?"

"I would, but Cindy could tell how upset he was that you weren't here, so she took him to get a soda. They'll be back in a minute."

"I'll be there inside of five." He wiped his eyes. It was no use pretending the federal agents looking at him weren't aware something significant was going on.

"Ranger Sims just came in and informed Beth you're on your way back in the helicopter. Please hurry."

"You can count on it," he vowed before clicking off. Right then she sounded as if she was anxious to see him, too, but maybe it was wishful thinking. His emotions were so off the charts, he couldn't trust anything.

For the next couple of minutes he chatted with the agents. After they landed, he said goodbye before racing toward the visitor center in the distance. He let himself in the back entrance.

Ranger Thompson came around the corner and stopped him. "Chief? We just got the word the quake set off a small rock slide at North Dome on the Tenaya Canyon side. I've checked, and there are no registered hikers in the immediate area affected."

Registered being the operative word. "Send a couple of teams up pronto. I'll authorize an air search before it gets too dark."

"Yes, sir."

Coming back from Porcupine Creek was like maneuvering a minefield, but every thought left his mind when he hurried down the hall and saw Nicky. The boy stood outside the door to Beth's office, waiting for him.

"Hey, sport!" Vance called out.

Nicky turned in his direction. "Vance!" He lunged for him. Vance doubted those six-year-old feet even touched the ground. The clasp of those arms around his neck felt so right, he couldn't love him more if he were his own flesh and blood. "Did you feel the earthquake, too?"

"No. I was flying in the helicopter." After rocking him for a long moment, he set him down. "Rachel told me there were waves in the tub."

Shining hazel eyes looked up at him. "You should have seen them. They were huge!"

"They were," she concurred.

He lifted his head and was impaled by a pair of brilliant green eyes. Rachel had come into the hall looking for Nicky. In a peppermint-pink shell top and white pleated pants, she looked good enough to eat.

"We're glad you're back," she declared in a husky voice.

"The feeling's mutual, believe me." In another second he was going to grab her in front of anyone who happened to be around, and never let go. "Stay with Beth while I finish up some last-minute business, then I'm all yours."

Giving Nicky's shoulder a squeeze, he disappeared into his office and phoned air rescue. "We've got to get up to the North Dome stat. Is the largest chopper available?"

"Yes, sir."

"Let's take it up, just in case we have injuries. I'll meet you at the helipad in ten minutes."

After another phone call to Mark, who was in charge as of now, Vance hurried back to Beth's office. Rachel's eyes flew to his. "Done already?"

He nodded. "Let's go."

"Goody!" Nicky ran out in the hall. Rachel hurried after him.

Vance glanced at Beth. "Thanks for taking care of...them." He'd almost said "my family." "Mark has taken over until further notice. Talk to you later."

She eyed him speculatively before he joined the two waiting for him. "We'll leave through the rear door."

He'd purposely taken them out the back way, where he kept the truck. Once he'd helped them inside, he climbed behind the wheel.

"Are we going to your house now?" Nicky asked eagerly.

"We sure are." It only took a minute to reach it. He pressed the remote above the visor and they entered the

garage. Quickly he got out and ushered them through
the laundry room into the kitchen.

"Now that you're here, I want you to make yourselves at home."

Chapter Ten

Rachel sensed immediately something was wrong. Vance didn't remove his hat. She darted him a glance. "Do you have to leave?"

"I'm afraid so, and I don't know how long I'll be. There's plenty of food in the fridge."

Nicky looked as crushed as she felt. "Where are you going?"

Vance hunkered down in front of him. "All the reports around the park have come in. The quake triggered one small rock slide at the North Dome. We don't think anyone was nearby, but as a precaution, I have to fly up there with Chase and take a look around. It's not far."

Nicky stared at him. "You think some rocks fell on people?"

His expression turned grim. "I hope that didn't happen."

"If you find them, will you carry them in the helicopter?"

Rachel's eyes closed tightly for a moment as she remembered what he'd done for Ben and Michelle, what he did every time there was a crisis. It took a special type of man to do what he did for a living and enjoy it.

"Yes," he replied in his deep voice. He hugged Nicky

hard before letting him go. "If I don't get back in time, we'll light those snakes in the morning." He flicked his gaze to Rachel. "In any event, I want you to stay here tonight. There are beds for everyone."

"We're going to sleep here?" Nicky's expression had brightened.

"Nowhere else."

"Goody! Hurry back!"

"You know I will." Vance high-fived him and stood up. His blue eyes searched Rachel's with new intensity. "I'll call you."

She nodded. "We'll be fine while you're gone. Take care," she urged, unable to prevent the quiver in her voice.

He stared hard at her. "I was just going to say that to you."

Within seconds he was gone. When they heard the sound of the motor, Nicky let out a sigh. "I wish he didn't have to leave."

"So do I, but that's the life of a ranger." She put her purse on the counter. "I'll fix dinner for us."

"Can I have a hot dog?"

"I'll look and see if he has some. Why don't you go find the bathroom and wash your hands? Then we'll eat."

"Okay."

After he bounded away, she made a quick call to her parents to let them know she and Nicky were fine. News of the quake would be all over the media. To her relief they hadn't heard yet, and were glad she'd phoned to prepare them.

Once they'd hung up she examined the contents in the fridge. Besides a stash of root beer, she found some frozen corn dogs. Nicky loved them. She did, too. There were apples and peaches in a bowl on the counter.

As she started to microwave the corn dogs, Nicky came running into the kitchen. "Look! This is Katy." He shoved a framed eight-by-ten picture at her.

"Nicky...you shouldn't have gone in Vance's bedroom."

"I didn't. This was in the living room."

"H-how do you know this is his wife?" Her voice faltered.

"'Cause he showed me a picture of her from his wallet." *He still carried it around?* Rachel groaned. "Don't you want to see it?"

No. But her curiosity over the woman he'd married won out, drawing Rachel's attention to the photograph. His redheaded wife was adorable. That she'd been full of personality and fun loving leaped from the picture. Rachel could well understand why Vance had never been able to move on.

Pain shot through her heart. "Put it back please, darling, then come and eat."

"Okay."

With a trembling hand she sliced up the fruit. When the corn dogs were done, she prepared their plates and put them on the table.

She heard Nicky's cry before he entered the kitchen again. "I found Timberwolf! Guess where he was?"

"I can't imagine."

"By the remote in the living room."

"I bet Vance knew Timberwolf was missing you, and left him out so you'd see him. Why don't the two of you sit down and eat."

"Okay. But Timberwolf doesn't like human food."

"Then how does he live?"

"They eat special pills on his planet."

"Ugh—that doesn't sound very fun. How sad he'll never taste a corn dog."

Nicky laughed. "You're silly, Mommy. I mean, Rachel."

She lurched in place. "That's okay. You can call me Mommy if you want."

He stared up at her with a sober expression. "Do you think my mommy would be mad if I called you that?"

Tears welled in Rachel's eyes. "No, because she knows how much I'd like to be your new mommy."

"You would?"

It was hard to swallow. "Yes."

"But I wasn't your baby."

"No, but I feel like you're my boy. I love you."

"I love you, too. I told Vance I wanted to call you Mommy."

Well, if he'd told Vance, then let it be written, let it be done. "I'd like you to call me that whenever you want to."

While they sat in Vance's house eating his food, she found herself loving the whole scene way too much. This was exactly like playing house. When she was little, she and the girl next door must have played it for hours a day. There was always a mommy and a child who waited for the daddy to come home from work.

But she'd never played ranger house. This was different. The daddy didn't come home at five o'clock on the dot, nor did he wear a suit and tie. If you were the mommy in this house, you were lucky to see him coming and going. In between times your heart ached while you waited and waited....

"RACHEL?"

Vance's low voice roused her from a light sleep. She sat up on the couch, shoving the hair out of her eyes.

He stood near the coffee table, but in the dim light of the living room, his body was a mere silhouette.

"Hi. How long have you been home?"

"I just walked in."

"What time is it?"

"After eleven."

She swung her feet to the floor. "Were there any people hurt tonight?"

"No."

"Thank heaven." She stirred restlessly. "In case you were wondering, Nicky's asleep in the guest bedroom."

"I figured as much." He picked up the photograph she'd seen earlier and sat down on the chair next to the couch. Maybe it didn't go on the coffee table.

"Nicky brought that to me earlier. Your wife was lovely."

"She was."

"How long has she been gone?"

"Five years." That long, and he still wore his ring? It was like another dagger to Rachel's heart. "We were very happy."

"Obviously," she whispered. "Did you try for a family?"

"No. We met in Germany while we were both in the military. I'd been injured and was flown there for treatment. She was one of my nurses. After eighteen months of marriage she was killed by a bomb while being deployed in the Middle East."

"I'm so sorry, Vance. I can't even comprehend it."

"At the time, I couldn't, either. I'm afraid we both

thought there'd be a future with children, but it didn't happen. As soon as I'd done my stint, I came back to the States and signed on with the rangers first in Colorado, then Utah. My goal was to end up here so I could help take care of my grandmother, who'd become an invalid."

Rachel nodded. "I know what that's like. My father's a virtual invalid because of a bad heart he's had all his life."

"*All* his life?" Vance sounded shocked.

"Yes. Last week his doctor told him of a new technology that could map it and find the problem to correct. He's considering having the surgery. It could change his life. On the other hand, if it doesn't work he could die on the operating table. If he decides to have it done, I need to be there."

"In other words, it's elective."

"Yes."

"What if he had the surgery in California, and could convalesce with you here? Your parents could move here permanently."

He was still talking about her taking the job he'd offered her? Her pain was too much. "I'm afraid it wouldn't work. They've each lived in Miami all their lives. To leave their friends, their memories... It just isn't feasible."

"Granted, all that is important, but you and Nicky are their lives. With your brother and his wife gone, nothing's more important than that."

She eyed him frankly. "You're right, but I still couldn't ask that of them at their age."

"They couldn't be that old. What's the real reason you're so hesitant?" Heat crept up her neck into her face. "Is it a matter of finances?"

"No. I appreciate your concern, but I don't want to talk about it anymore, if you don't mind."

"Forgive me. It's insensitive of me not to remember this is the place where Nicky lost his parents. Naturally, it has memories I'm sure you and your parents would rather forget."

"That's not it. I love it here. There's a majesty to this valley. At night the granite landmarks were even more awesome. After the humidity of Florida, I love the cool dry air at this elevation. You live in paradise."

"But I'm making you uncomfortable talking about it."

Rachel stood up from the couch to put distance between them. "You're not. I think the quake upset me a lot more than it did Nicky. The thought of my dad having to experience one in his condition makes the idea of moving here out of the question."

Now Vance was on his feet. "When are you taking Nicky back to Miami?"

"Day after tomorrow."

"Does he know that?"

"Yes. He had another bout with tears tonight before he fell asleep. Dr. Karsh said to make the vacation long enough to let Nicky feel like he'd been on one, but not too long to get the wrong idea."

"What's going to happen when he expects to come on another one next month?"

Vance already knew the answer to that question. Why was he trying to upset her like this? "I can't honestly answer that question. I told Nicky next spring, but I realize that sounds like a hundred years away. Excuse me for a minute. I want to check on him."

She hurried out of the living room and down the hall to the guest bedroom, so she wouldn't break down in front of him. To her shock, Nicky wasn't in bed. Maybe he was in the bathroom. She went across the hall, but he wasn't there, either.

"Nicky?" she called out. "Where are you, honey?" Rachel swung around. Vance had just come from his bedroom. "Is Nicky in your room?"

A CHILLING HAND SEEMED to squeeze Vance's heart. "No. I just checked." He rushed toward Rachel and clasped her upper arms. "When did you put him down?"

"At eight, but I don't think he fell asleep before eight-thirty." She looked terrified. "Where would he be?" She sounded as frantic as Vance felt.

"He can't be far," he stated. "We'll find him."

Vance got on the phone to Chase, to begin a massive search of the village, starting with the immediate area. After he hung up, he turned to Rachel. "When you talked about going home, that's when he must have decided to go into hiding. It's the typical thing a boy his age would do."

She nodded. "I'm sure you're right."

"Earlier today Nicky told me he wanted to live with me. I swear we'll find him, Rachel."

"Where do you think he could be hiding? It's been dark for several hours."

"While Chase coordinates the search, help me check the house."

They covered the entire place, looking under beds, inside closets and cupboards, anything he might climb or squeeze into. The hamper. They checked everything: the garage, the inside of the car and trunk.

"He's not here. Oh, Vance!"

He crushed her against him. "Shh..." He kissed her

forehead and temple. "He has to be nearby. At night, when he doesn't know the park, he'd have to stay close."

On their outing to the Tuolumne Meadows, Vance had emphasized how careful Nicky needed to be about black bears, but he kept those thoughts to himself now.

She slowly eased out of his arms. Her face glistened with tears. "I knew Nicky was determined to stay with you, but I didn't think he would go this far."

"It's what you do when you love someone."

"I know." Her voice shook. "He lost his daddy here. It appears he refuses to lose you, too. I shouldn't have brought him back."

"That's your fear talking. He's familiar with the lodge and could be hiding there. We'll drive over and look. Come on."

When they backed the car out, Ranger Baird was already stationed in front of the house, coordinating a search of the grounds within the housing complex. The men had orders to check all garbage cans and Dumpsters. He told Vance he'd stay put and keep an eye out for Nicky in case he decided to come back home.

With that arranged, Vance drove them to the lodge and found two more rangers combing the halls and foyer for Nicky. He hadn't turned up yet.

"Maybe he's in the dining court," Rachel cried.

"We'll check it out."

Together they talked with every waiter and waitress. So far no one had seen him. The pool was closed, but they covered every inch of the area, including changing rooms, bathrooms and receptacles.

"Come on, Rachel. We'll drive over to headquarters, where the rangers will be checking in."

A few minutes later, Vance let them in through the

back door and ushered her down the hall into his office. Beth followed them in with two mugs of hot coffee. She put them on the desk before hugging Rachel's shoulders. "Don't you worry. The guys will find our little junior ranger."

"I know. Thank you, Beth."

While Rachel sat in one of the chairs, struggling to hold on to her emotions, Vance went around his desk and phoned Chase. He turned his back toward her. "What's going on?"

"The entire Yosemite Valley has been put on alert. Every vehicle is being checked, including the trunks. Every hotel, every concession that's still open."

"What would I do without you?" he muttered to Chase. "If anything happens to him…"

"It won't. We'll find him."

"I know." He cleared his throat. "Keep me posted."

When he hung up and turned around, Rachel was staring up at him, teary eyed. "Any word yet?"

"No, but not all the rangers have reported in. Drink your coffee. Beth always makes it with a lot of sugar. You need it."

Rachel was too pale. His heart quaked in alarm.

She did his bidding and sipped a little of it before putting the mug down. "I just don't know what to do anymore. I thought Dr. Karsh had given me the right advice, but to have it end like this—I couldn't bear it if anything happened to him. I couldn't bear it!" Her agony reverberated in the room.

Neither could Vance. "Nothing's going to happen. What we need to do is decide what you're going to say to him when we do find him. Obviously, a vacation to the park next spring won't be soon enough for him. To be honest, it's not soon enough for me, either. I love that boy with all my heart."

Rachel buried her face in her hands. "That makes two of us."

She was shivering. Afraid she was going into shock, Vance hurried over to his closet to get a blanket off the shelf. He'd make her put her feet up on the chair, and wrap her up in it.

That's when he saw a telltale open root beer can on the floor next to his rubber boots.

His breath caught as he moved the long yellow mackintosh hanging above them. Crouched behind it was the most beautiful sight he'd ever seen. Two hazel eyes gazed up at him, clearly anxious, as if their owner was wondering how Vance would respond.

He hunkered down. "Hi, sport."

Vance heard Rachel's gasp, and felt her come up behind him.

"Hi." Nicky looked up at Rachel. "Are you guys mad at me?" he asked in a quiet little voice.

"No," Vance answered. "Do you want to tell us why you've been hiding?"

He nodded. "Because Rachel said we have to go home day after tomorrow. I don't want to go. I want to live here."

"Mind telling me how you got into my office without anyone seeing you, sport?"

"I waited out in back until one of the rangers opened the door to go in. He didn't know I sneaked in behind him."

"That was very resourceful. You're sounding like a ranger already."

"I want to be one! When nobody was looking, I ran to your office and hid in here. Is it okay if I took a root beer out of the fridge? I was thirsty."

Vance laughed for joy. Thank heaven for root beer! Without it, who knew how long Nicky would have stayed in there until he couldn't stand it any longer. "I bought it for you. Anything in my fridge is yours. Come here, son."

The boy climbed into his arms. While they hugged, Vance stood up and turned to Rachel, whose color was returning. Nicky reached to hug her. All three of them had their arms around each other when Beth walked in on them.

Her eyes rounded. "Where did our junior ranger come from?"

Nicky turned to her. "I hid in the closet."

"You mean you were in there all the time while everyone was worrying about you?"

"Yup."

"Well, all's well that ends well."

"Exactly," Vance concurred. "Beth, will you please phone Chase and tell him to call off the search?"

She beamed. "That's one order I'll gladly obey."

"You mean you haven't been glad about all the orders I issue around here?"

"I'll never tell."

He laughed again before focusing his attention on the two most important people in his life. "You know what, sport? I haven't had dinner yet. Let's all go home. I could eat a horse."

"How about an elephant?"

Vance started down the hall, still carrying him. "I could eat a gorilla."

"What about a bear?"

Rachel beat them to the rear door and opened it for them. "I'm sorry, guys, but the only thing we're serving this evening is corn dogs."

"I had two for dinner already, Mommy," Nicky said sleepily. He began to doze against Vance's shoulder.

"C'mon, sport. It's time to go home!"

An hour later, after Nicky had fallen asleep in the guest bedroom, Vance walked Rachel out to the living room. "Does he call you Mommy often?"

"Never until tonight. It thrilled me."

"Of course it would."

"I'm sorry Nicky's disappearance interfered with the rangers' work."

"A ranger's duty is to do whatever needs doing within the park boundaries. For a few hours tonight, their job was to find one little six-year-old boy."

Her eyes filled. "*You* were the one who found him."

"Only by chance. I was afraid you were going into shock. That's why I went to the closet for a blanket. You'll never know the joy I felt when I saw that empty can on the floor."

"You could never imagine my euphoria when I heard you say, 'Hi, sport.'" She sat down on the couch. "Vance? We're both exhausted. Go to bed and we'll talk in the morning." She couldn't handle any more togetherness right now.

"I'm going. We're going to need our sleep for the hike I have planned tomorrow."

As she pulled the light blanket over her, her eyes met his. "Thank you for finding him."

He brushed his hand against her cheek. "He'd have made his presence known eventually."

"I'm thankful it was sooner. That was your doing. Good night."

"Good night."

He left the living room experiencing a contentment

he hadn't felt in years creep through him. Everyone he cherished was beneath his roof tonight. His only fear now was that Rachel might not want the permanent position he hadn't discussed with her yet.

Chapter Eleven

Rachel couldn't hold back her feelings for the beauty of her surroundings. Standing at the edge of the forest, she saw undulating carpets of wildflowers, containing every hue from white, yellow, pink, red, blue and lavender, as far as the eye could see.

After flying to the Tuolomne Meadows Campground, Vance had taken them hiking to one of his favorite sections of high alpine terrain.

They had left their fishing gear along the bank of the nearby stream, and walked out to the meadow.

"This can't be real!" Rachel cried, so entranced she ran forward, laughing for pure joy. Nicky followed her and started rolling around. She followed suit and grabbed for him. Together they lay on their backs, out of breath, and looked up at an impossibly blue sky sparsely dotted with cotton white clouds.

"Nicky, darling? Have you ever in your life seen a more beautiful spot?"

"Nope." He pointed to the clouds. "They look like pillows!"

"Big fat ones!"

"Yeah."

While they studied their shapes, Vance stretched out his hard-muscled length beside her, his right hand propping up his head. With his left he held a yellow, cup-shaped flower under her nose, seducing her with its sweet fragrance. It looked tiny in his strong, bronzed hand.

His ring finger stood out because of the band of white skin exposed there. He wasn't wearing his wedding ring. Taken totally by surprise, Rachel was slow to compute what it meant. When the significance caught up to her, she turned her head in his direction.

What she saw in those blue eyes trained on her was a look of such unbridled desire it deprived her of breath. She lay there in disbelief as he lowered his head and covered her mouth with his own. It happened so naturally, she welcomed him the way she did the sun warming their bodies.

He didn't have to coax a response from her. With an eagerness born of her profound love for him, she opened her mouth to the urgent pressure of his. Lying among the wildflowers, she was conscious only of her thundering heart and the whirr of insect wings as their kiss deepened and took on a life of its own. Rapture such as she'd never known spread through her being. If this soaring feeling could go on forever...

"Vance? How come you're kissing Rachel?"

Delirious from the passion he'd aroused, she was much slower to respond than the man who'd set her on fire. He lifted his head with seeming reluctance, leaving her bereft.

"Because I felt like it." His voice held a smoky tinge, betraying the extent of his involvement.

"Oh." Nicky stood looking down at them. "When are we going to go fishing?"

"In a few minutes. Why don't you see if you can find a butterfly? We don't have many in the park lately. See how many you can count. It's very important."

"Okay. I'll be right back."

"There's no hurry. We've got all afternoon."

Rachel was afraid to move or say anything for fear she was having a dream and might wake up.

"Now where were we?" Vance murmured. Once again his mouth found hers. Without an audience, neither one of them could contain their eagerness to be in each other's arms. He rolled over on his back, pulling her on top of him, crushing her against him while he gave in to the needs he'd been holding back since they'd first met.

She was with him all the way. While his hands roved over her back, she kissed every portion of his face, then returned to his mouth. Her hunger matched his, practically giving him a heart attack in the process.

Knowing Nicky would be back any minute, he moved her so they lay side by side. His desire for her was escalating out of control. Kissing her lovely features, he cried, "I'm in love with you, Rachel. Do you hear me? You're the most beautiful thing in my life. The only reason I didn't say something sooner was because of Steven. I had to be sure you were really over him."

Her eyes burned a flaming hot green. "I was afraid that was why. I've been dying for you to give me a clue. Oh, Vance, you've become my whole world, my life! I love you so much, you can't imagine…"

"Yes, I can, because I'm in the same state." He cupped her face in his hands and drank deeply from her mouth. When he finally relinquished her lips, he said,

"I need you in my life. When you left the park before, I didn't know how I was going to make it."

She ran kisses along his jaw. "As you can see, I came right back, because I couldn't stay away."

He rolled her on her back to kiss her again, but no kiss was long enough or deep enough. Now that the floodgates were open, life was pouring in again, the part that had been missing for so many years.

"Hey, Vance? I can't find any butterflies!"

Rachel kissed his throat. "Don't tell him the truth."

"What do you mean?"

"Since you confessed that you love me, all the butterflies have been flying around inside of me."

He gave her one more urgent kiss, but nothing could assuage his deep hunger for her.

Nicky ran up to them. "How come you're still kissing her?"

"Because I love it!"

"Oh." Nicky stood looking down at them.

Vance sat up and smiled at the boy who'd climbed into his heart and was permanently lodged there. "Didn't you see even *one* butterfly?"

"Not any."

A disheveled Rachel got to her knees, looking like a woman who'd been kissed senseless.

"When are we going to go fishing?"

"Right now, sport." Vance sprang to his feet. Rachel grabbed the hand he extended to help her stand up, but her whole body was trembling, and he knew it.

THANK GOODNESS SHE COULD blame her glowing cheeks on the sun's rays, Rachel thought. Flushed and aroused, she headed for the pines.

Nicky ran to catch up with her. "Do you like it when he kisses you?" he asked.

She chuckled. Up to now Nicky hadn't thought outside the box where his relationship with Vance was concerned. The kissing he'd observed had opened the lid, never mind that it had shaken her to the foundations and changed her entire universe.

"I love it, just the way I love it when you decide to give me one."

Having easily caught up to them, Vance winked at her before grasping Nicky's shoulder. As they walked ahead, she followed at a short distance, watching them interact. A boy with his hero, both wearing T-shirts and jeans.

Rachel hadn't thought anything could improve on nature, but she had to concede there wasn't anything as perfect as two beautiful males discussing the merits of a rainbow trout over a brown.

Deep in the forested area, the undergrowth of purple lupine was so lush it almost hid the stream in spots. Vance pointed out wonderful round rocks big enough to stand or sit on for the best fly-fishing angle.

"Hey!" Nicky cried out. "Where's our fishing stuff?"

His question jerked Rachel from her intimate thoughts, and she looked around. Sure enough, their rods, plus a tackle box holding a few drinks and treats, were nowhere to be found. Her gaze flew to Vance, whose black brows met above the piercing blue of his eyes as he frowned.

"It looks like we had unwanted company." He whipped out his cell phone.

A chill ran down her spine to think someone had been spying on them, waiting for the right moment to disappear with their equipment.

Her eyes probed his. "Do you think it was someone from the campground?"

"Probably," he murmured, but she had a feeling he was entertaining another possibility. Vance wasn't the chief for nothing. He knew everything that went on in the park.

"No matter what, they couldn't be far away yet, since they'd have to be on foot," she theorized.

"You're right."

She heard him start talking to security as he walked a little ways off. Whatever was on his mind, he didn't want to alarm them.

Nicky stayed by Rachel's side with a troubled look in his eyes. He'd been so looking forward to going fishing. One of those poles had been a gift from Vance's grandfather. None of it was fair. Not on this glorious day.

Vance soon pocketed his phone and came back to them. "Tell you what, Nicky. I have more gear at the house. Tomorrow morning we'll go fishing up in the Hetch Hetchy Valley, where Chief Sam used to take me, and catch ourselves some big ones."

The boy's lower lip quivered. "Do we have to go home now?"

"I'm afraid so. Some park business has come up I have to take care of personally. But after you freshen up at the lodge, we can do anything you want. There's a stargazing show at Glacier Point, or we can drive to Wawona and visit the pioneer village."

"Can we go back to your house and eat dinner?"

"Of course." Vance flicked his gaze to Rachel for approval. The longing in his eyes told her that was his choice, too. Her heart raced as she nodded.

The three of them started to retrace their steps. Nicky

took hold of Vance's hand and they headed down to the lower meadow.

"Whoever took our stuff was *mean*. They stole your flies."

"Yup, but they're not going to get away with it, because I want my present back," Vance vowed with ferocity. Again Rachel got the impression he knew a lot more than he was telling.

"When you catch them, I think you should put them in jail!"

"They'll go to jail all right. Then the federal judge will sentence them to prison."

A shudder ran through Rachel. Vance *did* know something.

THE SECOND VANCE WALKED into the holding cell cabin, Chase made a beeline for him.

"Sorry to ruin your outing with Rachel, but Mark and I want you to take a look at the four guys we caught with your gear."

"Did you recover all of it?"

He nodded.

"Did they ruin it?"

"No."

"That's good. I intend to give Nicky the pole my grandfather gave me. Where did you pick them up?"

"Above that area where you found the first plantings of marijuana. We discovered they've been spotted around the campground on and off for a couple of months. When I asked to see their fishing licenses, they couldn't produce them. I examined their gear and recognized your tackle box."

"This means four more culprits we've put away.

We're wiping out that bunch. You do great work, Chase. You were on them before they could destroy my property. I owe you more than you know."

His friend looked at Vance's ringless finger and grinned. "Yeah?"

"I'll tell you about *that* later."

"I'm holding you to it. Now for unpleasant issues. Before the feds get here, go in and see if you can identify any of these guys. If you do, we'll be able to add more prison time to their final sentencing."

Vance was perplexed. "You think I've seen them before?"

"I don't know. While we cuffed them one muttered something to his cohort about being glad the chief ranger wasn't around to recognize him."

"That's interesting. I'll take a look."

Ranger Baird unlocked the door so Vance could walk down the hall to the holding area.

Four miscreants were held in two cells. The one he'd caught in a hammerlock in the pool stood out. He glared at Vance in hatred. Earlier, Vance had assumed they were college students doing too much drinking. But these no-accounts were working for a sophisticated outfit growing marijuana. It was dangerous business. He was thankful they were behind bars. The thought of any of them hurting Rachel or Nicky put him in a rage.

He walked back out to join Chase. "Bingo."

"Yeah?"

Vance proceeded to tell him about the incident at the pool before he signed his statement. "Call in the lifeguard from the lodge for a statement. He'll make a positive identification, too."

"Excellent." Chase walked outside with the fishing

gear he'd recovered, and put it in the back of Vance's car. Then he looked Vance in the eye. "You seem different."

"This afternoon I told her I was in love with her."

His friend smiled ear to ear. "And?"

He took a deep breath. "She's in love with me, too."

"There was never any question. With the ring gone I figured you'd get to first base in a hurry. As Beth whispered to me this morning, the whole park's going to breathe easier once the news is out. She's known Rachel was nuts about you from the beginning."

Vance clapped a hand on his shoulder. "Thanks. You know what I mean."

"I couldn't be happier. You three were meant to be together."

"One day it's going to happen to you."

"Let's take it one bachelor at a time, shall we? I live in hope that once Nicky is legally yours, he might end up liking his uncle Chase. Now go on home to your family. See ya later, *alligator.*"

The comment caused Vance to chuckle. He got in his car and broke the speed limit to get there. When he opened the garage with the remote and pulled in, Nicky came bounding out the laundry-room door to greet him. This was a new experience, one Vance had been aching for when he thought he'd never have children.

They hugged, then Nicky said, "Come on in. We've made a nummy dinner."

"I can't wait. What are we having?"

"Hot dogs and fruit salad."

"Perfect. Guess what? I got all our fishing stuff back. Tomorrow we'll try out the new flies you gave me."

"Goody!"

Seeing his golden-haired Rachel in the kitchen gave

Vance another heart attack. She smiled at him, melting him on the spot.

"Hi. Give me five minutes," he murmured.

"We're glad you're back."

"You don't know the half of it."

No man ever showered or dressed faster. He joined them at the kitchen table, and she watched while he dug into his food. "Nicky said you recovered your gear."

"Good old Chase. He always gets his man. The place would fall apart without him. There's no one like him."

"I agree. He's a terrific man."

"I guess I don't need to tell you how he feels about you."

She blushed. "If I hadn't met you first..."

Vance smiled into her eyes. "That wasn't our best moment."

"Rachel was mad," Nicky interjected.

"At me?"

"Yup."

Vance chuckled. "Chase thinks you don't like him."

"Yes, I do," Nicky stated.

"Maybe you should tell him sometime," Rachel suggested.

"Okay." He finished the last piece of melon. "Can we play a game now? Rachel brought over Match Up."

"I've never heard of it, but it sounds fun. First, however, I have a very important question to ask you. I want you to think very hard before you answer."

Nicky's cute little face started to look worried. "What is it?"

Vance's heart was skidding all over the place. "What would you think if Rachel and I got married?"

The shadows disappeared. "Oh, that. I want you to," he said promptly.

"But you didn't even think about it."

"Yes, I did. When we went home, I told Papa and Nana."

Vance could see Rachel's eyes shimmering. He was so humbled he could hardly talk.

Nicky studied both of them. "Will you be my new mommy and daddy?"

"Yes." Rachel spoke at last. "We'd be your new parents."

"'Cause my old parents died, huh."

Vance couldn't take much more. "I love you, sport. I'd give anything to be your daddy."

"I want you to be!" He flew into Vance's arms.

Over the boy's blond head Vance stared at Rachel. "Then it's settled?"

"Yes. I love you, Chief Rossiter. I want to marry you. I can't wait."

Nicky finally let go of him and ran around the table to hug her. "How soon are we getting married? Tomorrow?"

She laughed through her tears. "Oh, no, darling. A lot of things have to be worked out first."

"But we're going to stay here, huh."

"Yes. Of course, we have to discuss everything with Nana and Papa."

"I wish they lived here, too."

Vance got to his feet. "That can be arranged. You know my house in Oakhurst?"

"Yup."

"Maybe you can talk them into living in it after your papa has his operation. That way you can visit them all the time."

Nicky's smile lit up the room. "And they can stay at our house sometimes."

Our house. Incredible.

"They can come anytime they want."

By now Vance had reached Rachel and pulled her into his arms. He searched her eyes. "I love you. You do know this is forever."

"It better be. I want your babies. Nicky is going to need siblings."

"Anything to oblige." Vance kissed her long and hard, wanting to get started on their marriage this very second. But it wasn't the time or the place. "Let's call your parents."

"They're going to be so happy."

"I'm the one who's happy," Vance whispered against her lips.

When he felt Nicky's arms wrap around their legs, the significance of Chief Sam's vision hit him full force, filling him with wonder.

After ten springs, we found three fledgling gray owls near the edge of the meadow yesterday. A big change is coming for you.

* * * * *

Watch for Chase's story,
THE RANGER'S SECRET,
coming September 2009,
only from Harlequin American Romance!

ALEXANDROS KAREDES, snow dusting the shoulders of his leather jacket and glittering like jewels in his dark hair, stood at the door. Maria felt the blood drain from her head.

"Good evening, Ms. Santos."

His voice was as she remembered it. Deep. Husky. Perfect English, but with the faintest hint of a Greek accent. And cold, as cold as it had been that awful morning she would never forget, when he'd accused her of horrible things, called her terrible names....

"Aren't you going to ask me in?"

She fought for composure. Last time they'd faced each other, they'd been on his turf. Now they were on hers. She was in command here, and that meant everything.

"There's a sign on the door downstairs," she said, her tone every bit as frigid as his. "It says, 'No soliciting or vagrants.'"

His lips drew back in a wolfish grin. "Very amusing."

"What do you want, Prince Alexandros?"

A tight smile eased across his mouth and it killed her that even now, knowing he was a vicious, arrogant man, she couldn't help but notice what a handsome mouth it was. Chiseled. Generous. Beautiful, like the rest of him, which made him living proof that beauty could, indeed, be only skin deep.

"Such formality, Maria. You were hardly so proper the last time we were together."

She knew his choice of words was deliberate. She felt her face heat; she couldn't help that but she damned well didn't have to let him lure her into a verbal sparring match.

"I'll ask you once more, your highness. What do you want?"

"Ask me in and I'll tell you."

"I have no intention of asking you in. Tell me why you're here or don't. It's your choice, just as it will be my choice to shut the door in your face."

He laughed. It infuriated her but she could hardly blame him. He was tall—six-two, six-three—and though he stood with one shoulder leaning against the door frame, hands tucked casually into the pockets of the jacket, his pose was deceptive. He was strong, with the leanly muscled body of a well-trained athlete.

She remembered his body with painful clarity. The feel of him under her hands. The power of him moving over her. The taste of him on her tongue.

Suddenly, he straightened, his laughter gone. "I have not come this distance to stand in your doorway," he said coldly, "and I am not going to leave until I am ready to do so. I suggest you stand aside and stop behaving like a petulant child."

A petulant child? Was that what he thought? This man who had spent hours making love to her and had then accused her of—of trading her body for profit?

Except it had not been love, it had been sex. And the sooner she got rid of him, the better.

She let go of the doorknob and stepped aside. "You have five minutes."

He strolled past her, bringing cold air and the scent of the night with him. She swung toward him, arms folded. He reached past her, pushed the door closed, then folded his arms, too. She wanted to open the door again but she'd be damned if she was going to get into a who's-in-charge-here argument with him. She was in charge, and he would surely see a tussle over the ground rules as a sign of weakness.

Instead, she looked past him at the big clock above her worktable.

"Ten seconds gone," she said briskly. "You're wasting time, your highness."

"What I have to say will take longer than five minutes."

"Then you'll just have to learn to economize. More than five minutes, I'll call the police."

Instantly, his hand was wrapped around her wrist. He tugged her toward him, his dark-chocolate eyes almost black with anger.

"You do that and I'll tell every tabloid shark I can contact about how Maria Santos tried to buy a five-hundred-thousand-dollar commission by seducing a prince." He smiled thinly. "They'll lap it up."

* * * * *

What will it take for this billionaire prince to realize he's falling in love with his mistress…?
Look for
BILLIONAIRE PRINCE, PREGNANT MISTRESS
by Sandra Marton
Available July 2009
from Harlequin Presents®.

We'll be spotlighting a different series every month
throughout 2009 to celebrate our 60th anniversary.

Look for Harlequin® Presents in July!

TWO CROWNS, TWO ISLANDS, ONE LEGACY

A royal family, torn apart by pride and its lust for
power, reunited by purity and passion

Step into the world of Karedes
beginning this July with

BILLIONAIRE PRINCE,
PREGNANT MISTRESS
by

Sandra Marton

Eight volumes to collect and treasure!

You're invited to join our Tell Harlequin Reader Panel!

By joining our new reader panel you will:

- Receive Harlequin® books—they are FREE and yours to keep with no obligation to purchase anything!
- Participate in fun online surveys
- Exchange opinions and ideas with women just like you
- Have a say in our new book ideas and help us publish the best in women's fiction

In addition, you will have a chance to win great prizes and receive special gifts!
See Web site for details. Some conditions apply.
Space is limited.

To join, visit us at
www.TellHarlequin.com.

REQUEST YOUR FREE BOOKS!
2 FREE NOVELS PLUS 2
FREE GIFTS!

American ★ Romance®

Love, Home & Happiness!

YES! Please send me 2 FREE Harlequin® American Romance® novels and my 2 FREE gifts (gifts are worth about $10). After receiving them, if I don't wish to receive any more books, I can return the shipping statement marked "cancel." If I don't cancel, I will receive 4 brand-new novels every month and be billed just $4.24 per book in the U.S. or $4.99 per book in Canada.* That's a savings of close to 15% off the cover price! It's quite a bargain! Shipping and handling is just 50¢ per book. I understand that accepting the 2 free books and gifts places me under no obligation to buy anything. I can always return a shipment and cancel at any time. Even if I never buy another book from Harlequin, the two free books and gifts are mine to keep forever.

154 HDN EYSE 354 HDN EYSQ

Name	(PLEASE PRINT)	
Address		Apt. #
City	State/Prov.	Zip/Postal Code

Signature (if under 18, a parent or guardian must sign)

Mail to the **Harlequin Reader Service**:
IN U.S.A.: P.O. Box 1867, Buffalo, NY 14240-1867
IN CANADA: P.O. Box 609, Fort Erie, Ontario L2A 5X3

Not valid to current subscribers of Harlequin® American Romance® books.

Want to try two free books from another line?
Call 1-800-873-8635 or visit www.morefreebooks.com.

* Terms and prices subject to change without notice. Prices do not include applicable taxes. N.Y. residents add applicable sales tax. Canadian residents will be charged applicable provincial taxes and GST. Offer not valid in Quebec. This offer is limited to one order per household. All orders subject to approval. Credit or debit balances in a customer's account(s) may be offset by any other outstanding balance owed by or to the customer. Please allow 4 to 6 weeks for delivery. Offer available while quantities last.

Your Privacy: Harlequin is committed to protecting your privacy. Our Privacy Policy is available online at www.eHarlequin.com or upon request from the Reader Service. From time to time we make our lists of customers available to reputable third parties who may have a product or service of interest to you. If you would prefer we not share your name and address, please check here. ☐

HAR09R

HARLEQUIN *Super Romance*

THE BELLES OF TEXAS

They're as strong as the state that raised
them. The Belle sisters aren't afraid to go
after what they want, whether it's reclaiming
their ranch or their family.

Linda Warren
CAITLYN'S PRIZE

Thanks to her deceased father's gambling
debts, Caitlyn Belle's beloved High Five Ranch
is in dire straits. Particularly because the
will stipulates that if the ranch doesn't turn
a profit in six months, it must be sold to
Judd Calhoun—the man Caitlyn jilted
fourteen years ago. And Cait knows Judd has
been waiting a long time for his revenge....

*Look for the first book
in The Belles of Texas miniseries,
on sale in July wherever books are sold.*

From *New York Times*
bestselling authors

CARLA NEGGERS
SUSAN MALLERY
KAREN HARPER

More Than Words:
STORIES OF STRENGTH

They're your neighbors, your aunts, your sisters and your best friends. They're women across North America committed to changing and enriching lives, one good deed at a time. Three of these exceptional women have been selected as recipients of Harlequin's More Than Words award. And three *New York Times* bestselling authors have kindly offered their creativity to write original short stories inspired by these real-life heroines.

Visit **www.HarlequinMoreThanWords.com**
to find out more, or to nominate
a real-life heroine in your life.

Proceeds from the sale of this book will be reinvested in Harlequin's charitable initiatives.

Available in March 2009 wherever books are sold.

SUPPORTING CAUSES OF CONCERN TO WOMEN ❖ HARLEQUIN
WWW.HARLEQUINMORETHANWORDS.COM

PHMTW668

INTRODUCING THE FIFTH ANNUAL
MORE THAN WORDS ANTHOLOGY

Five bestselling authors
Five real-life heroines

A little comfort, caring and compassion go a long way toward making the world a better place. Just ask the dedicated women handpicked from countless worthy nominees across North America to become this year's recipients of Harlequin's More Than Words award. To celebrate their accomplishments, five bestselling authors have honored the winners by writing short stories inspired by these real-life heroines.

Visit **www.HarlequinMoreThanWords.com**
to find out more, or to nominate
a real-life heroine in your life.

Proceeds from the sale of this book will be reinvested in Harlequin's charitable initiatives.

Available in April 2009 wherever books are sold.

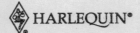

COMING NEXT MONTH
Available July 14, 2009

#1265 BACHELOR CEO by Michele Dunaway
Men Made in America

When Chase McDaniel learns his position has been usurped by
Miranda Craig, the CEO apparent is stunned. He's devoted his whole life
to the family business—it's his legacy. But the more he gets to know his
gorgeous replacement, the more he wants the job *and* the woman who's
standing in his way. Is there room at the top for both of them?

#1266 A FATHER FOR JESSE by Ann Roth
Fatherhood

Emmy Logan came to Halo Island with her son to make a fresh start. But
what her boy really needs is a man in his life—someone who'll stick around.
Mac Struthers is *not* that man. After raising his two brothers, the last thing he's
looking for is another family. So why is the rugged contractor acting as if that's
exactly what he wants?

#1267 LAST RESORT: MARRIAGE by Pamela Stone

Charlotte Harrington needs to get married—quickly! With her grandfather
looking at every move she makes managing one of his hotels and a slimy
ex-boyfriend on the scene, Charlotte is desperate. And a fake marriage with
playboy Aaron Brody seems a harmless way to buy her some time—until she
falls in love with him.

#1268 THE DADDY AUDITION by Cindi Myers

Tanya Bledso has returned to Crested Butte to raise her daughter and run the
local community theater. She expected to find the same quiet, quirky small
town—but the place is bustling! And it's Jack Crenshaw who's responsible for
this mess. Tanya will tell her former high school sweetheart what she thinks of
his *development*…as soon as she conquers the attraction between them!

www.eHarlequin.com

HARCNMBPA0609